Masterpieces of
SUSPENSE

Compiled by Rosamund Morris

D0840275

HART PUBLISHING COMPANY, INC.

New York City, New York

ACKNOWLEDGMENTS

Grateful acknowledgment is made to the copyright owners for permission to reprint the following stories:

"Blackmail" by Allan Vaughan Elston; copyright 1949 by The Crowell-Collier Publishing Co., reprinted by kind permission of Paul R. Reynolds, Inc.

"The Wooden Horse" by Eric Williams; copyright 1958 by Eric Williams, reprinted by kind permission of Abelard-Schuman, Ltd.

"The Fourth Man" by John Russell; copyright 1917 by P. F. Collier & Son, reprinted by kind permission of Brandt & Brandt.

"The Price of the Head" by John Russell; copyright 1916 by P. F. Collier & Son, reprinted by kind permission of Brandt & Brandt.

"The Man Who Liked Dickens" from *A Handful of Dust* by Evelyn Waugh; copyright 1944 by Evelyn Waugh, reprinted by kind permission of Little, Brown and Company.

"Remember the Night" by Day Keene; copyright 1941 by Popular Publications, Inc., reprinted by kind permission of Popular Publications, Inc.

"The Baby in the Icebox" by James M. Cain; copyright 1932 by James M. Cain, reprinted by kind permission of Harold Ober Associates.

"Miracle of the Fifteen Murderers" by Ben Hecht; copyright 1943 by Ben Hecht, reprinted by kind permission of Jacques Chambrun, Inc.

"Swindler's Luck" by Ben Hecht; copyright 1943 by Ben Hecht, reprinted by kind permission of Jacques Chambrun, Inc.

CONTENTS

Masterpieces of
SUSPENSE

BEN HECHT (1894-1964)

. . . was one of the most lively and versatile literary talents in America. He was born in New York of immigrant Russian parents, who moved to Chicago and then to Racine, Wisconsin, when Hecht was still a young boy. At sixteen he ran away from home and found himself a job on the Chicago Journal. *In 1914 he went to work for the Chicago* News *and became a part of the Chicago "renaissance" of the time, writing and publishing stories in the literary magazines. In the 20's he began publishing novels and writing plays, but his first big success did not come until 1930, when* Front Page, *written in collaboration with Charles MacArthur, was produced.*

Ben Hecht was active and successful in almost every field of writing—books, stories, movies, plays, television scripts.

The Sunset Kid had

SWINDLER'S LUCK

— in every way!

I KNEW HIM when he was called the Sunset Kid and also Moony Dan. The first name came to him because he used to drive to the Santa Monica beach late every afternoon and watch the sun go down. He said it made him lucky. And if there was ever a man who needed a lot of luck, it was the Sunset Kid. For the Kid was a crook who devoted himself to swindling members of the underworld.

He specialized in trimming big-shot bookies and professional card gamblers. Among these he was called a "thief," which is the name illegal gamblers righteously pin on any kind of con man. Yet knowing the Kid for a thief, they let him come around and swindle them year after year. They played cards with him and took his bets on horses, and even went in on deals with him —and always got trimmed.

The Kid prospered as a thief because not only luck but psychology was on his side. The psychology was the egoism of the big-shot crooks whom he swindled, plus the ennui in which they lived, plus their childlike interest in everything crooked.

They were wise guys who knew all the angles and who boasted that no thief could hang anything on them. The fact that the Kid constantly disproved this theory made them only eager for "a return match." And it was understood between the Kid and his victims that they would have to catch him only once. There was a lot of fascination in it for the suckers, watching a man fool them with his life at stake on a slip-up.

The name Moony Dan came to the Kid as a result of his unusual fondness for women. This is an uncommon trait among crooks, whose relation to women is likely to be crude and sketchy. Women are a minor trouble and a lesser delight in their lives.

It was otherwise with the Sunset Kid, alias Moony Dan. His love affairs had been always as important to him as his crimes. At thirty-five he was paying alimony to two ex-wives—a fact which made his underworld contacts regard him as a bigger sucker than any of the wise guys he fleeced.

"I don't pay them money because the law tells me to," the Kid told me. "I pay it because I owe it to them, on account of they once made me happy."

This was five years ago. I asked the Kid another question at that time. He was a good-looking physical specimen. I asked him how he had stayed out of the war.

"My heart," he said. "I've got a ticker that can't take much strain. Sometimes I've got to stay in bed for a couple of days at a time."

"Sorry to hear that," I said.

"It works out," the Kid smiled. "I get to do my practice—and figuring—that way." The practice, I learned, was with a deck of cards, and the figuring was a new swindle to work on the wise guys who were gunning for him.

I was with the Kid when he met Annie Bond, and I saw a thing happen that is seldom believeable when you read about it. I saw two people fall in love at first sight like a pair of cymbals coming together. It happened so quickly and reasonlessly that I thought they were both kidding for my benefit. It wasn't only love that sat down with us at that back table in the Mexican restaurant. Death also modestly introduced himself.

The Kid was always a neat, well-dressed fellow. He had a moody, somewhat sarcastic-looking face and a crop of curly black hair. I'd always thought him a normally attractive man. But looking at him as Annie Bond sat beside him, I saw a man of beauty. Emotion seemed to give him a new face.

I didn't know Annie well enough to know how deep or how novel was the look she turned on the Sunset Kid. In a girl of virtue and modesty, it would have been pretty convincing. But Annie was of another category. She was no tramp, for she worked hard for a living. As an entertainer in this somewhat shabby Mexican night spot, Annie sang twenty or thirty songs an evening, changed her costumes several times and did a few dance numbers.

But she was a girl who had had bad luck with men. Beginning when she was twenty, which was eight years before she looked at the Sunset Kid, she had always picked the wrong man or, rather, been picked by him.

She had come to Hollywood from Amarillo, Texas —red-haired and shapely, with a fair singing voice and a wagon-load of temperament. Her tops had been a few bit parts in the studios, and she had slid down from there. She sang in out-of-the-way cafés when she "got a break," she told me once. The rest of the time she clerked in stores or waited on tables or risked her life for fifty dollars a day as a stunt rider in a Western movie. She was good on a horse. And she had earned her own living every week of the eight years.

The bad luck in her love affairs came out of the fact that she attracted men who were weak and floundering around with a half talent and a half manhood. They were apt to be entertainers on the skids like herself, or idlers with an angle, or overdressed errand boys for mysterious big shots. There hadn't been too many, but there had been enough to make Annie Bond at twenty-eight, a far cry from the innocent who had left Amarillo. The red hair was still there and the shapeliness and the unafraid lift of her neck. But the eight years had left a dust on her heart and a sneer in her eyes.

I thought of this as I saw Annie Bond staring at the Sunset Kid ten minutes after I had introduced them. She didn't return the Kid's smile, and there was none of his radiance in her look. But something somber and faraway had come into her face that made her seem like someone just born.

I saw Annie Bond and the Sunset Kid four months later. A car honked at me as I was walking to my hotel in Beverly Hills. The Kid was behind its wheel, and Annie, her hair blowing in the wind, was beside him.

"Come on along," the Kid said. "We're taking a little ride to Santa Monica."

We reached the beach in time. The sun was resting like a red hoop on the horizon. We parked and the Kid watched it, almost as avidly as Annie Bond watched him. Her eyes were wide with love, and the eight Hollywood years were gone from her face.

The last red sliver of the sun dropped out of sight and the Kid smiled. "My lucky piece. I'm going to need it next week. . . . Mind if I tell him, Annie?"

Annie didn't mind.

"We're getting married," the Sunset Kid said. "On the fifteenth. Because fifteen is my lucky number. In the morning at ten-thirty. And at nine o'clock that night I'm going into business. Quittin' all my tricks and settling down as a regular citizen."

"He's buying a half-interest in The Congo Room," Annie's husky voice was eager. The Congo was one of Hollywood's newest night clubs, complete with name band, low-key lighting and a run of celebrities. "Dan's going to be the manager. And I'm going to sing there."

"In a silver gown with silver slippers," said the Kid. He took her hand and kissed it. "Her name'll be up in lights," he said. "Annie Bond, the Texas Nightingale."

"If I make good," said Annie.

"You've made good," the Kid said softly.

"I'm so dizzy I don't know if I'm comin' or goin'," said Annie. "Imagine something like this happening to me! I don't mean my name in lights. I mean Dan."

"To both of us," Dan smiled. "That's why I'm quittin' the tricks. They used to be the only fun there was. Now they don't mean anything."

I thought of some questions.

"Buying in on the Congo is going to require a bank roll, isn't it?"

"Ten grand, cash," he answered.

"Have you got it?" I asked.

"I'm getting it on the fifteenth," the Sunset Kid smiled.

Seven men sat in Rocky Blair's elegant living room. Three of them were bodyguards, three were Rocky's friends and assistants. The seventh was Rocky. Six were in shirt sleeves, collars undone. It was one P.M., June fifteenth, and the day was hot.

Rocky was having his breakfast on a tray. He was fully and resplendently dressed, as became a king, regardless of the hour or temperature. Rocky's empire consisted of five hundred bookies—and several unallied and legal enterprises which he ran as a sort of hobby.

Chief among these was the Boulevard Florist Shop in the center of Hollywood. It was in the rear of the rambling, sweet-scented establishment that Rocky had his "home office."

Out of this aromatic chamber Rocky operated his five hundred bookies. For guiding them financially, delivering them out of bondage when the police grew fractious, and smoothing their ways with the juices of bribery and corruption in high and low places, Rocky pulled down an average of a hundred thousand dollars each week.

There was no syndicate involved. There was only Rocky, sitting, as he sat this hot day, as the one and only king of the territory between Los Angeles and Las Vegas.

Rocky was a finicky man with a round, tight face that nobody had ever seen unshaved. He had, despite the elegance of his attire, the look of a well-barbered pugilist sitting in his corner between rounds with motionless, determined eyes, and lips pinched together—and waiting. The posture and expression came naturally to him, for he had sat in a ring corner as a pugilist during five of his youthful years.

Rocky sat in silence with his six guests as he drank his coffee. The three bodyguards were mugs with nothing to say. The three assistants, more capable of conversation, specialized in being as tight mouthed as their boss.

A musical gong sounded three times. It was the front doorbell. Rocky continued sipping his coffee and nobody moved. The gong sounded again, and Rocky looked at Gil, the smallest of the bodyguards, but who wore a gun and holster near his left armpit, visible only when his coat was off, as now.

Gil stood up and moved to the front door. Two attempts to wipe out Rocky Blair had been made that month.

The six listened to the outer door open. There were no shots and no bomb came rolling into the room, from which they knew that this was a social caller.

Gil re-entered the silent room.

"It's that Moony Dan," he said.

"What's the thief want?"

"To see you, Rocky," said Gil.

"Throw him out," said the fat-faced Tubby Fields, who was considered Rocky's "brains." "Don't waste any time."

"Shut up," said Rocky. Everybody waited a full minute, and then Rocky concluded his speech, "Show the gentleman in."

Gil went into the hallway again and undid the two steel chains on the door. He returned leading the Sunset Kid.

Nobody spoke. Rocky peered out of the living-room window into the street beyond the wide front lawn.

"You got no car," said Rocky.

"I came in a taxi," the Kid said.

"On purpose, eh?" Rocky scowled. "What the hell for?"

"I felt lucky," the Sunset Kid answered.

All seven men in the room put on the same expression. It was an expression of indifference. And all seven felt the same lift of excitement. The Kid had announced openly that he had come to steal money again from Rocky Blair.

"Throw him out," said Tubby Fields.

Nobody moved and the Kid sat down. Rocky finished his coffee. Anger fumed in his eyes. This monkey had taken him three times—once in a poker game in this same room. With seven guys watching every move of the thief's fingers, and putting a fresh deck of cards into play every fifteen minutes, this trimmer had taken him for twenty-eight hundred dollars. And all in the last pot, which was the way he always worked. You got four kings and he came up with his signature— four aces—and blew.

"I ain't playin' cards," said Rocky.

"Glad to hear it," said the Kid. "Takes too long to make a killing at cards. Sometimes you have to sit around for hours."

"I make the suggestion a thoid time," said Tubby Fields. "Throw this fella out."

Rocky scowled at his "brains." Usually he followed Tubby's advice. Tubby, he always said, had a "fourth sense." He knew things in advance. But Rocky didn't want to throw the kid out. It would be a confession of weakness, and, besides, how could a thief trim him in his own house with seven guys watching his every move?

"I'm doin' this," Rocky answered Tubby. "So shut

up." Turning to his visitor, he added, "what kind of play do you want?"

"I feel lucky on the horses today," said the Kid.

All seven in the room, including even Tubby Fields, were glad nobody had thrown the visitor out—because this was going to be something good. The Kid was going to try to pull a "past-post" betting gag on the boss, right under their noses. That was different from pulling it on the lugs behind the bookie counters.

All seven remembered, in a minimum of words, the Kid's work as a betting thief. He had made a lot of cleanups placing bets after a race was over, and betting on a horse that had already won. One of the simpler ways he had used was calling up three minutes before a race had started and putting down bets on the race that was going to follow. There was a girl taking the bets. And the Kid would keep on talking to the girl over the phone, telling her some story he had found out, about her sister, and offering to help get the sister out of some trouble she was in. And then, all of a sudden, he would say, "Put five hundred on Sun Up to win in the second." The girl taking the bets would forget to look at the clock because she was excited over the Kid saving her sister, and she would mark down: "Sun Up—$500—Second Race." And the second race would be already run and over.

The Kid would come around at five to collect his winnings, and the girl would be fired.

There were other tricks the Kid had worked. Rocky remembered them all, including the "invisible-ink" trick. The Kid had handed in a betting slip with the names of three horses on it to win the third, fourth and fifth races. On the slip was also written the name of a horse that had already won the first race. But it was written in invisible ink. The bookie couldn't see it when he filed the betting slip. By five o'clock, when the Kid came around to collect, the invisible ink had "come up" and become visible. And the bookie had to pay off on a horse that had been bet on after he had won the race.

Tubby had figured that one out, but there was no proving it. And you couldn't knock a guy off without catching him guilty. This was the unwritten law in Rocky's kingdom just as it was the written law outside it.

Not only Rocky but all the others here in Rocky's home knew every past-post betting gag that had ever been pulled. And all seven went to work at once. That is, they alerted themselves.

"Sit over here," said Tubby Fields. He moved the Sunset Kid away from the front window overlooking the wide lawn and arranged his chair so that the visitor's back was to it. There would be no signaling from outside.

Nate, the oldest and wisest bookie among Rocky's retainers, opened the window and looked out. Rocky's house stood in a sparsely built and would-be fashionable neighborhood. There was no house on its immediate left or right. The street was wide and there were no houses of any sort on the opposite side.

Rocky looked at the clock on the mantelpiece. It was 1:10.

"You got some nag picked?" Rocky asked.

He winked at Tubby, and Tubby winked back. The others also winked at one another.

The Kid looked at the seven men all now openly studying his hands, feet and face. A rueful smile turned his mouth.

"I like Count Monty in the first," he said, "but I haven't made up my mind yet."

"You want a little more time, eh?" Rocky sneered. Count Monty was running at 1:30.

"That's right," said the Kid. "Do you mind if I use your bathroom, Mr. Blair?"

"Go right ahead," said Rocky. "There's one in the hallway."

"Yes, I know," the Kid said. He stood up and started out of the room. At a nod from Rocky, two of his guests also stood up and followed the Kid as far as the bathroom door. They remained outside.

"He ain't gonna try," said Gil, a little regretfully. "You scared him off, Rocky."

"He'll try," said Tubby Fields.

"Naw," Rocky grinned coldly. "He was feelin' big when he came in here. He ain't feelin' so big now."

"Too bad," one of the heavy guards said. "We could 'a' caught him."

"He's gonna try," Tubby repeated.

"Okay," said Rocky. "Then we'll catch him. I been wantin' to catch that thief a long time."

Inside the bathroom, the Sunset Kid turned the key in the lock and smiled to himself. He knew the talk that was being made in the room he had left. He knew that Tubby Fields was on the telephone getting the right time and setting his watch by it, and the clock on the mantelpiece. One-thirty would be one-thirty in Rocky's living room, the same as it was in the rest of California, including the Santa Anita Race Track.

But the Kid was smiling at something more important going on in the room he had left—its psychology. He knew that at 1:33, one minute after the first race at Santa Anita had been run, Rocky would take his bet—on the horse that had won.

The Kid switched on the electric light over the medicine cabinet, turned on both faucets to cover the sound, and then unscrewed the electric bulb. He sighed as he worked. He was glad this was his last trick—just this one for Annie—nothing else. He removed the tin-foil lining from a package of cigarettes and shaped it into a penny-sized disk. Placing the tin foil in the socket, he screwed the bulb tightly into place.

There was a faint pop, and the Kid knew a fuse in some basement box had been blown. He unscrewed the bulb again and removed the tin foil. He had knocked out the bathroom current, and the odds were twenty to one that the adjoining living room was on the same fuse.

If it was, he was "in business." If it wasn't—the Kid shrugged mentally—he would have to dream up another gag. He made a deep wish. "Annie, make it work," he muttered. Then he rinsed his hands quickly, turned off the water and opened the door.

"You're sittin 'here," said Tubby Fields as the Kid preceded the bodyguards into the living room. "The same chair."

The Kid sat down.

Rocky looked at the clock. It was 1:17.

"You made up your mind yet?" he asked.

"I think I'll skip the first race," the Kid smiled.

Rocky's face stiffened and darkened.

"We ain't taking bets after starting time," Tubby Fields said quietly. "Don't try pullin' any."

"Shut up," Rocky said. "I'm concentratin'." His eyes, tense and angry, were on the Kid's face.

"It's one-twenty-five," said Tubby after a long silence.

"Okay," said Rocky, "turn on the radio. We'll catch the first race."

Biggy, one of the guards, stepped to the radio cabinet. Nobody watched him. All eyes remained on the thief.

"No bets after the race starts," said Rocky. "This is your last chance. You want to make a play?"

"I don't feel it," said the Sunset Kid.

"Hell!" Biggy was muttering. "This thing ain't workin'."

Hearing Biggy's words, the Sunset Kid relaxed. He knew he was "in business." The rest was psychology.

"What ain't workin'?" Rocky asked irritably.

"The radio," said Biggy. "He's knocked it out."

"Who's knocked it out?" Rocky kept his eyes on the visitor.

"The Kid," said Biggy.

"He ain't touched it," said Rocky firmly. "Get the set out of my bedroom. Hurry up."

Tubby Fields stood up and cried out harshly. "He's done it, I tell ya! The gag is on! Throw him out!"

"He's done nothin'," said Rocky. "I been watchin' him. Shut up now."

Biggy returned with a smaller radio set and plugged it into a light socket. Rocky looked at the mantelpiece clock. It was 1:30.

"This one don't work either," Biggy growled. "He's busted this one likewise."

The Kid's eyes were on Tubby Fields. He waited for the "brains" to call the shot—a blown fuse. But the "brains" was too busy watching to think. Besides, the Kid was gambling that the theory of fuse boxes was unknown to the assemblage.

"Is the wire cut?" one of Rocky's aides asked.

"The wire's okay," said Biggy. "There's somethin' the matter inside. It don't even go on."

Dimly, Rocky was aware that this was a feint of some kind, and he kept his eyes on every flick of the thief's eyes.

"That's too bad," said the Sunset Kid. "I would have liked to hear that race run. I had a hunch on Count Monty. But I'm glad I didn't bet. Because I got a bigger hunch right now, a real feeling. Blue Skies. Care to take a bet on Blue Skies, Mr. Blair?"

Rocky looked at the clock. It was 1:33. The first race had ended a minute ago—if they'd got away quick.

"I'll put three thousand on Blue Skies to win," said the Sunset Kid. "It's no different playing my hunch now than ten minutes ago. You don't know and I don't know what's happened."

As he talked, the Kid removed six five-hundred-dollar bills and put them on the breakfast tray at Rocky's elbow.

"You taking my bet?" he asked.

Rocky's hand reached for the money. "I'm taking that bet," he said.

The room was silent. There had been no signal. The thief had sat in the middle of the room, his back to the street fifty feet beyond. Tubby waddled to the phone and called a number. The room waited for his announcement.

"Tubby Fields," said Tubby huskily into the mouthpiece. "Gimme the results in the first at Santa Anita."

He listened and hung up slowly.

"Blue Skies by a nose," he announced. "Paid seven to two."

"You dirty thief," Rocky said. "You've stole ten grand off me."

"I didn't steal it," said the Sunset Kid softly. "I won it."

"You stole it," Rocky repeated. His hand moved slowly under his coat. He was forgetting the unwritten law.

"If you want to welsh on a bet you took," said the

Kid, "go ahead. You don't have to shoot me. You just don't pay off."

Rocky's hand stopped moving. A gambler couldn't do anything against that kind of talk. It was an easy psychology play from here in, and the Kid kept all smugness out of his voice.

"You made the bet after looking at the clock," he said. "But if you feel you've been taken, in your own house, with all your smart pals watching me, you don't have to pay. That's up to you, Mr. Blair."

"I'm payin'," said Rocky.

He took ten thousand-dollar bills out of his wallet.

"I'll give you five more," he said quietly, "if you tell me how you done it."

The Kid smiled at the trap. "I got a feeling all of a sudden," he answered naïvely. "It came a little late, but it was a genuine feeling."

He took the bills from Rocky's hand and picked up his own three thousand. The others watched and were silent.

"You're a lousy thief," said Rocky, without emotion. "You never won an honest nickel in your life. I'm payin' off, because I took the bet with my eyes open. But I'm gonna get the money back. I'm gonna find out what kind of a gag you pulled. And when I find out, I'm comin' after you. And you won't need no money after that."

The Sunset Kid waited patiently for Rocky to finish his long, slow speech.

"I'm sorry you've got that attitude, Mr. Blair," he

said. "But thanks for payin' off."

He nodded, added, "So long," and walked slowly out of the room.

Outside in the bright afternoon, the Sunset Kid walked toward a boulevard intersection two blocks distant. As he turned the corner he glanced back to see if anyone had followed him. The blazing street was empty of all life.

Four automobiles were lined up, one behind the other, at the boulevard curb. It was an odd collection of cars. The oddity lay in their coloring. One was black, one bright green, one red, and the fourth was a salmon yellow.

The Sunset Kid thought of the fifth and missing car, the light blue one. He resavored for a moment the thrill of catching a glimpse of it in the mirror over Rocky's mantelpiece, watching the bit of blue flash by. He had even noted in that brief swing across the mirror that Annie's hair was flying and her face grinning. She had flashed by at a good seventy.

The mystification of the seven men and the almost foolish simplicity of the gag kept the Kid grinning as he got into the red car. There had been five horses running in the first race. Each of the different colors of the five cars represented one of the running horses. Annie had sat getting the race over the car radio. As soon as the winner was called, Annie had jumped into the right car—the blue one for Blue Skies.

The Kid drove the red job to the car-rental garage out of which he had taken it three days ago. He returned an hour later to the boulevard curb and the three other rented cars. One by one, he restored them to their widely separated garage headquarters.

It was nearly seven when the Kid had returned the last of the four rentals. He was weary and hot with driving. A quick look at the sky told him he was on schedule. He would be able to get to the beach in Santa Monica in time to watch the sun go down, with Annie. She would be waiting, parked at their usual front-row seat for the sunset, in the blue car.

There was no blue car parked when the Sunset Kid rolled up to the beach end of the street. He shut off the motor and sat staring at the sun going down.

Annie would drive up any minute. Annie had gone to buy something—a hot dog or sunburn lotion. The sun seemed to take a long time going down. The Kid tried to breathe casually. Annie would show. What were a few minutes of waiting? There was a whole life of Annie ahead now. The Kid turned on the car radio. Time passed faster when music was playing. It was seven-thirty and the Kid hit a new broadcast and let it run.

Suddenly he took his eyes from the setting sun. He closed them and looked at nothing. The newscaster's voice filled the car.

"Los Angeles counted its one hundred and fortieth victim of reckless driving this afternoon. A car speeding along at seventy miles an hour down a Brentwood residential street crashed into a parked delivery truck. The driver of the car was killed instantly. Her name was Annie Bond, a young and beautiful café singer known as the Texas Nightingale."

When the Sunset Kid opened his eyes, the Pacific was dark. His hands were shaking and he couldn't move his legs to start the car. He laid his head on the wheel and cried.

Three days later, the Sunset Kid walked into Rocky Blair's Boulevard Flower Shop. A heavy-set colored man with a cauliflower ear was behind the main counter. He stared at the Kid and said nothing.

Biggy looked up from a picture magazine he was reading. He also said nothing, but walked to a door at the rear of the flower shop. He pressed a button three times. The heavy steel door opened.

"That fella's here," said Biggy. "That Moony Dan."

Rocky Blair came out, followed by Tubby Fields. Rocky went behind the flower counter. Biggy and Tubby took a place on each side of the Kid.

"I read about your girl," said Rocky. "She was killed in an accident after drivin' a blue car past my house. Around one-thirty."

The Kid nodded.

"I been lookin' for you," said Rocky. He stared at the white face and the bloodshot eyes in front of him and asked harshly, "What do you want?"

"I want to buy some flowers," the Kid said.

"We're wastin' time," said Tubby. "Take him into the office, Biggy."

"Shut up," Rocky scowled. "I'm waitin' on a customer. . . . What kind o' flowers do you want, Kid?"

"Roses," said the Sunset Kid. "I want fifteen dollars' worth of roses sent every week to Miss Annie Bond. She's buried in Forest Lawn. I want the roses put on her grave every week for the next fifteen years. That'll be about ten grand. And seven hundred extra. I'm paying in advance."

The kid put ten one-thousand dollar bills on the counter and added another seven hundred.

"That'll cover it," he said. "And if you sell the business or anything happens, I'd like to fix it so the delivery keeps on."

Rocky Blair looked at the shaking hands and the bleared eyes in front of the counter.

"Mr. Fields will enter your order," said Rocky stiffly. "The flowers will be delivered as specified." He paused, scowled and added, "Take care of the man, Tubby, and give him a receipt." And Rocky walked back into his steel-doored office.

When I go to the Santa Monica beach, I stop in at an oyster bar that faces the ocean. It's a small and rather sloppy place, and the sea food is none too good. But I go there for a meal now and then because Dan Flato waits on me. He used to be called the Sunset Kid.

His hands are still shaking and his eyes have kept the bleary look that came to them one time when he watched the sun go down. But the Kid doesn't watch the sun any more. He has a new hobby. When he waits on me his eyes look across the counter toward the street end where Annie Bond was going to meet him—that time.

MIRACLE OF THE FIFTEEN MURDERERS

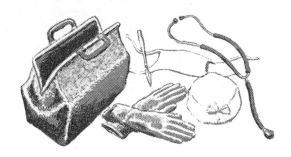

THERE IS ALWAYS an aura of mystery to the conclaves of medical men. One may wonder whether the secrecy with which the fraternity surrounds its gatherings is designed to keep the layman from discovering how much it knows, or how much it doesn't know. Either knowledge would be unnerving to that immemorial guinea pig who submits himself to the abracadabras of chemicals, scalpels, and incantations under the delusion he is being cured rather than explored.

Among the most mysterious of medical get-togethers in this generation have been those held in New York City by a group of eminent doctors calling themselves the X Club. Every three months this little band of healers have hied themselves to the Walton Hotel, overlooking the East River, and behind locked doors and beyond the eye of even medical journalism, engage themselves in unknown enterprise lasting till dawn.

What the devil had been going on in these conclaves for twenty years no one knew, not even the ubiquitous head of the American Medical Association, nor yet any of the colleagues, wives, friends, or dependents of the X Club's members. The talent for secrecy is highly developed among doctors, who, even with nothing to conceal, are often as close-mouthed as old-fashioned bomb throwers on their way to a rendezvous.

How, then, do I know the story of these long-guarded sessions? The answer is—the war. The war has put an end to them, as it has to nearly all mysteries other than its own. The world, engaged in re-examining its manners and its soul, has closed the door on minor adventure. Nine of the fifteen medical sages who comprised the X Club are in uniform and preside over combat-zone hospitals. Deficiencies of age and health have kept the others at home—with increased labors. There is a part of science which retains a reluctant interest in the misfortunes of civilians and has not yet removed its eye entirely from the banal battlefields on which they ignominiously keep perishing.

"Considering that we have disbanded," Dr. Alex Hume said to me at dinner one evening, "and that it is unlikely we shall ever assemble again, I see no reason for preserving our secret. Yours is a childish and romantic mind, and may be revolted by the story I tell you. You will undoubtedly translate the whole thing into some sort of diabolical tale and miss the deep human and scientific import of the X Club. But I am not the one to reform the art of fiction, which must substitute sentimentality for truth, and Cinderella for Galileo."

And so on. I will skip the rest of my friend's all-knowing prelude. You may have read Dr. Hume's various books, dealing with the horseplay of the sub-conscious. If you have, you know this bald-headed master mind well enough. If not, take my word for it, he is a genius.

There is nobody I know more adept at prancing around in the solar plexus swamps, out of which most of the world's incompetence and confusion appear to rise. He has, too, if there is any doubt about his great talent, the sneer and chuckle which are the war whoop of the super-psychologist. His face is round and his mouth is pursed in a chronic grimace of disbelief and contradiction. You can't help such an expression once you have discovered what a scurvy and detestable morass is the soul of man.

Like most subterranean workers, my friend is almost as blind as a bat behind his heavy glasses. And like many leading psychiatrists, he favors the short and stocky or balloonlike physique of Napoleon.

The last dramatic meeting of the X Club was held on a rainy March night. Despite the hostile weather, all fifteen of its members attended, for there was an added lure to this gathering. A new member was to be inducted into the society.

Dr. Hume was assigned to prepare the neophyte for his debut. And it was in the wake of the round-faced soul fixer that Dr. Samuel Warner entered the sanctum of the X Club.

Dr. Warner was unusually young for a medical genius—that is, a recognized one. And he had never received a fuller recognition of his wizardry with saw, ax, and punch hole than his election as a member of the X Club. For the fourteen older men who had invited him to be one of them were leaders in their various fields. They were the medical peerage. This does not mean necessarily that any layman had ever heard of them.

Eminence in the medical profession is as showy, at best, as a sprig of edelweiss on a mountaintop. The war, which offers, its magic billboards for the vanities of small souls and transmutes the hunger for publicity into sacrificial and patriotic ardors, has not yet disturbed the anonymity of the great medicos. They have moved their bushels to the front lines and are busy under them, spreading their learning among the wounded.

The new member was a tense and good-looking man with the fever of hard work glowing in his steady, dark eyes. His wide mouth smiled quickly and abstractedly, as is often the case with surgeons who train their reactions not to interfere with their concentration.

Having exchanged greetings with the eminent club members, who included half of his living medical heroes, Dr. Warner seated himself in a corner and quietly refused a highball, a cocktail, and a slug of brandy. His face remained tense, his athletic body straight in its chair, as if it were poised for a sprint rather than a meeting.

At nine o'clock Dr. William Tick ordered an end to all the guzzling and declared the fifty-third meeting of the X Club in session. The venerable diagnostician placed himself behind a table at the end of the ornate hotel room and glared at the group ranged in front of him.

Dr. Tick had divided his seventy-five years equally between practicing the art of medicine and doing his best to stamp it out—such, at least, was the impression of the thousands of students who had been submitted to his irascible guidance. A Professor of Internal Medicine at a great Eastern medical school, Dr. Tick had favored the Education by Insult theory of pedagogy. There were eminent doctors who still winced when they recalled some of old bilious-eyed, arthritic, stooped Tick's appraisals of their budding talents, and who still shuddered at the memory of his medical philosophy.

"Medicine," Dr. Tick had confided to flock after flock of students, "is a noble dream and at the same time the most ancient expression of error and idiocy known to man. Solving the mysteries of heaven has not given birth to as many abortive findings as has the quest into the mysteries of the human body. When you think of yourself as scientists, I want you always to remember that everything you learn from me will probably be regarded tomorrow as the naïve confusions of a pack of medical aborigines. Despite all our toil and progress, the art of medicine still falls somewhere between trout casting and spook writing.

"There are two handicaps to the practice of medicine," Tick had repeated tenaciously through forty years of teaching. "The first is the eternal charlatanism of the patient who is full of fake diseases and phantom agonies. The second is the basic incompetence of the human mind, medical or otherwise, to observe without prejudice, acquire information without becoming too smug to use it intelligently, and, most of all, to apply its wisdom without vanity."

From behind his table old Tick's eyes glared at the present group of "incompetents" until a full classroom silence had arrived, and then turned to the tense, good-looking face of Dr. Warner.

"We have a new medical genius with us tonight," he began, "one I well remember in his pre-wizard days. A hyperthyroid with kidney disfunction indicated. But not without a trace of talent. For your benefit, Sam, I will state the meaning and purpose of our organization."

"I have already done that," said Dr. Hume, "rather thoroughly."

"Dr. Hume's explanations to you," Tick continued coldly, "if they are of a kind with his printed works, have most certainly left you dazed if not dazzled."

"I understood him quite well," Warner said.

"Nonsense," old Tick said. "You always had a soft spot for psychiatry and I always warned you against it. Psychiatry is a plot against medicine. And who knows but it may someday overthrow us? In the meantime, it behooves us not to consort too freely with our enemies."

You may be sure that Dr. Hume smiled archly at this.

"You will allow me," Tick went on, "to clarify whatever the learned Hume has been trying to tell you."

"Well, if you want to waste time." The new member smiled nervously and mopped his neck with a handkerchief.

Dr. Frank Rosson, the portly and distinguished gynecologist, chuckled. "Tick's going good tonight," he whispered to Hume.

"Senility inflamed by sadism," said Hume.

"Dr. Warner," the pedagogue continued, "the members of the X Club have a single and interesting purpose in their meeting. They come together every three months to confess to some murder any of them may have committed since our last assembly. I am referring, of course, to medical murder, although it would be a relief to hear any of us confess to a murder performed out of passion rather than stupidity. Indeed, Dr. Warner, if you have killed a wife or polished off an uncle recently, and would care to unbosom yourself, we will listen respectfully. It is understood that nothing you say will be brought to the attention of the police or the A. M. A."

Old Tick's eyes paused to study the growing tension in the new member's face.

"I am sure you have not slain any of your relatives," he said, sighing, "or that you will ever do so except in the line of duty.

"The learned Hume," he went on, "has undoubtedly explained these forums to you on the psychiatric basis that confession is good for the soul. This is nonsense. We are not here to ease our souls but to improve them. Our real purpose is scientific. Since we dare not admit our mistakes to the public and since we are too great and learned to be criticized by the untutored laity and since such inhuman perfection as that to which we pretend is not good for our weak and human natures, we have formed this society. It is the only medical organization in the world where the members boast only of their mistakes.

"And now"—Tick beamed on the neophyte—"allow me to define what we consider a real, fine professional murder. It is the killing of a human being who has trustingly placed himself in a doctor's hands. Mind you, the death of a patient does not in itself spell murder. We are concerned only with those cases in which the doctor, by a wrong diagnosis or by demonstrably wrong medication or operative procedure, has killed off a patient who without the aforesaid doctor's attention, would have continued to live and prosper."

"Hume explained all this to me," the new member muttered impatiently, and then raised his voice; "I appreciate that this is my first meeting and that I might learn more from my distinguished colleagues by listening than by talking. But I have something rather important to say."

"A murder?" Tick asked eagerly.

"Yes," said the new member.

The old professor nodded. "Very good," he said. "And we shall be glad to listen to you. But we have several murderers on the docket ahead of you."

The new member was silent and remained sitting bolt upright in his chair. It was at this point that several, including Hume, noticed there was something more than stage fright in the young surgeon's tension. The certainty filled the room that Sam Warner had come to his first meeting of the X Club with something violent and mysterious boiling in him.

Dr. Philip Kurtiff, the eminent neurologist, put his hand on Warner's arm and said quietly, "There's no reason to feel bad about anything you're going to tell us. We're all pretty good medical men, and we've all at one time or another done worse—whatever it is."

"If you please," old Tick demanded, "we will have silence. This is not a sanatorium for doctors with guilt complexes. It is a clinic for error. And you will continue to conduct it in an orderly, scientific fashion. If you want to hold Sam Warner's hand, Kurtiff, that's your privilege. But do it in silence."

He beamed suddenly at the new member.

"I confess," he went on, "that I'm as curious as anybody to hear how so great a know-it-all as our young friend Dr. Warner could have killed off one of his customers. But our curiosity will have to wait. Since five of you were absent from our last gathering I think that the confession of Dr. James Sweeney should be repeated for your benefit."

Dr. Sweeney stood up and turned his lugubrious face and shining eyes to the five absentees. Of all present, Sweeney was considered next to old Tick the ablest diagnostician in the East.

"Well," he said in his preoccupied monotone, "I told it once, but I'll tell it again. I sent a patient to my X-ray room to have a fluoroscopy done. My assistant gave him a barium meal to drink and put him under the fluoroscope. I walked in a half-hour later to observe progress, and when I saw the patient under the fluoroscopic screen, I observed to my assistant, Dr. Kroch, that it was amazing and that I had never seen anything like it. Kroch was too overcome to bear me out, and remained utterly speechless.

"What I saw was the patient's entire stomach and lower esophagus were motionless and dilated, apparently made out of stone. And as I studied this phenomenon, I noticed it was becoming clearer and sharper. The most disturbing factor in the situation was that we both knew there was nothing to be done. Dr. Kroch, in fact, showed definite signs of hysteria. Shortly afterward, the patient became moribund and fell to the floor."

"Well, I'll be damned!" several of those who had been absent cried in unison; Dr. Kurtiff adding, "What was it?"

"It was simple," said Sweeney. "The bottom of the glass out of which the patient had drunk his barium meal was caked solid. We had filled him up with plaster of Paris. I fancy the pressure caused a fatal coronary attack."

"Good Lord," the new member said. "How did it get into the glass?"

"Through some pharmaceutical error," said Sweeney mildly.

"What, if anything, was the matter with the patient before he adventured into your office?" Dr. Kurtiff inquired.

"The autopsy revealed chiefly a solidified stomach and esophagus," said Sweeney. "But I think from several indications that there may have been a little tendency to pyloric spasm, which caused the belching for which he was referred to me."

"A rather literary murder," said old Tick. "A sort of Pygmalion in reverse."

The old professor paused and fastened his red-rimmed eyes on Warner. "By the way, before we proceed," he said, "I think it is time to tell you the full name of our club. Our full name is the X Marks the Spot Club. We prefer, of course, to use the abbreviated title as being a bit more social sounding."

"Of course," said the new member, whose face now appeared to be getting redder.

"And now," announced old Tick, consulting a scribbled piece of paper, "our first case on tonight's docket will be Dr. Wendell Davis."

There was silence as the elegant stomach specialist stood up. Davis was a doctor who took his manner as seriously as his medicine. Tall, solidly built, gray-haired, and beautifully barbered, his face was without expression—a large pink mask that no patient, however ill and agonized, had ever seen disturbed.

"I was called late last summer to the home of a workingman," he began. "Senator Bell had given a picnic for some of his poorer constituency. As a result of this event, the three children of a steam fitter named Horowitz were brought down with food poisoning. They had overeaten at the picnic. The senator, as host, felt responsible, and I went to the Horowitz home at his earnest solicitation. I found two of the children very sick and vomiting considerably. They were nine and eleven. The mother gave me a list of the various foods all three of them had eaten. It was staggering. I gave them a good dose of castor oil.

"The third child, aged seven, was not as ill as the other two. He looked pale, had a slight fever, felt some nausea—but was not vomiting. It seemed obvious that he, too, was poisoned to a lesser degree. Accordingly, I prescribed an equal dose of castor oil for the youngest child—just to be on the safe side.

"I was called by the father in the middle of the night. He was alarmed over the condition of the seven-year-old. He reported that the other two children were much improved. I told him not to worry, that the youngest had been a little late in developing food poisoning but would unquestionably be better in the morning, and that his cure was as certain as his sister's and brother's.

"When I hung up, I felt quite pleased with myself for having anticipated the youngest one's condition and prescribed the castor oil prophylactically. I arrived at the Horowitz home at noon the next day and found the two older children practically recovered. The seven-year-old, however, appeared to be very sick indeed. They had been trying to reach me since breakfast. The child had 105 degrees temperature. It was dehydrated, the eyes sunken and circled, the expression pinched, the nostrils dilated, the lips cyanotic, and the skin cold and clammy."

Dr. Davis paused. Dr. Milton Morris, the renowned lung specialist, spoke. "It died within a few hours?" he asked.

Dr. Davis nodded.

"Well," Dr. Morris said quietly, "it seems pretty obvious. The child was suffering from acute appendicitis when you first saw it. The castor oil ruptured its appendix. By the time you got around to looking at it again, peritonitis had set in."

"Yes," said Dr. Davis slowly. "That's exactly what happened."

"Murder by castor oil." Old Tick cackled. "Plus an indifference to the poor."

"Not at all," Dr. Davis said. "All three children had been at the picnic, overeaten alike, and revealed the same symptoms."

"Not quite the same," Dr. Hume said.

"Oh, you would have psychoanalyzed the third

child?" Dr. Davis smiled.

"No," said Hume. "I would have examined its abdomen like any penny doctor, considering that it had some pain and nausea, and found it rigid with both direct and rebound tenderness."

"Yes, it would have been an easy diagnosis for a medical student," Dr. Kurtiff agreed. "But unfortunately, we have outgrown the humility of medical students."

"Dr. Davis' murder is morally instructive," old Tick announced, "but I find it extremely dull. I have a memo from Dr. Kenneth Wood. Dr. Wood has the floor."

The noted Scotch surgeon, famed in his college days as an Olympic Games athlete, stood up. He was still a man of prowess, large-handed, heavy-shouldered, and with the purr of masculine strength in his soft voice.

"I don't know what kind of murder you can call this." Dr. Wood smiled at his colleagues.

"Murder by butchery is the usual tickle," Tick said.

"No, I doubt that," Dr. Morris protested. "Ken's too skillful to cut off anybody's leg by mistake."

"I guess you'll have to call it just plain murder by stupidity," Dr. Wood said softly.

Old Tick cackled. "If you'd paid a little more attention to diagnosis than to shot-putting, you wouldn't be killing off such hordes of patients," he said.

"This is my first report in three years," Wood answered modestly. "And I've been operating at the rate of four or five daily, including holidays."

"My dear Kenneth," Dr. Hume said, "every surgeon is entitled to one murder in three years. A phenomenal record, in fact—when you consider the temptations."

"Proceed with the crime," Tick said.

"Well"—the strong-looking surgeon turned to his hospital colleague, the new member—"you know how it is with these acute gall bladders, Sam."

Warner nodded abstractedly.

Dr. Wood went on: "Brought in late at night. In extreme pain. I examined her. Found the pain in the right upper quadrant of the abdomen. It radiated to the back and the right shoulder. Completely characteristic of gall bladder. I gave her opiates. They had no effect on her, which, as you know, backs up any gall bladder diagnosis. Opiates never touch the gall bladder."

"We know that," said the new member nervously.

"Excuse me." Dr. Wood smiled. "I want to get all the points down carefully. Well, I gave her some nitroglycerine to lessen the pain then. Her temperature was 101. By morning the pain was so severe that it seemed certain the gall bladder had perforated. I operated. There was nothing wrong with her gall bladder. She died an hour later."

"What did the autopsy show?" Dr. Sweeney asked.

"Wait a minute," Wood answered. "You're supposed to figure it out, aren't you? Come on—you tell me what was the matter with her."

"Did you take her history?" Dr. Kurtiff asked after a pause.

"No," Wood answered.

"Aha!" Tick snorted. "There you have it! Blind-man's buff again."

"It was an emergency." Wood looked flushed. "And it seemed an obvious case. I've had hundreds of them."

"The facts seem to be as follows," Tick spoke up. "Dr. Wood murdered a woman because he misunderstood the source of a pain. We have, then, a very simple problem. What besides the gall bladder can produce the sort of pain that that eminent surgeon has described so clearly. Anyone care to speculate?"

"Heart," Dr. Morris answered quickly.

"You're getting warm," said Wood.

"Before operating on anyone with so acute a pain, and in the absence of any medical history," Tick went on, "I would most certainly have looked at the heart."

"Well, you'd have done right," said Wood quietly. "The autopsy showed an infraction of the descending branch of the right coronary artery."

"Which a cardiogram would have told you," said old Tick. "But you didn't have to go near a cardiograph. All you had to do was ask one question. If you had even called up a neighbor of the patient, she would have told you that previous attacks of pain came on exertion—which would have spelled heart, and not gall bladder.

"Murder by a sophomore," old Tick pronounced wrathfully.

"The first and last," said Wood quietly. "There won't be any more heart-case mistakes in my hospital."

"Good, good," old Tick said. "And now gentlemen, the crimes reported thus far have been too infantile for discussion. We have learned nothing from them other than that science and stupidity go hand in hand, a fact already too well known to us. However, we have with us tonight a young but extremely talented wielder of the medical saws. He has been sitting here for the last hour, fidgeting like a true criminal, sweating with guilt and a desire to tell all. Gentlemen, I give you our new and youngest culprit, Dr. Samuel Warner."

Dr. Warner faced his fourteen eminent colleagues with a sudden excitement in his manner. His eyes glittered, and the dusty look of hard work and near exhaustion, already beginning to mar his youth, lifted from his face.

The older men regarded him quietly and with various degrees of irritation. They knew, without further corroboration than his manner, that this medico was full of untenable theories and half-baked medical discoveries. They had been full of such things themselves once. And they settled back to enjoy themselves. There is nothing as pleasing to a graying medical man as the opportunity of slapping a dunce cap on the young of science. Old Tick, surveying his colleagues, grinned. They had all acquired the look of pedagogues holding a switch behind their backs.

Dr. Warner mopped his neck with his wet handkerchief and smiled knowingly at the medical peerage.

"I'll give you this case in some detail," he said, "because I think it contains as interesting a problem as you can find in practice."

Dr. Rosson, the gynecologist, grunted but said nothing.

"The patient was a young man, or rather a boy," Warner went on eagerly. "He was seventeen, and amazingly talented. He wrote poetry. That's how I happened to meet him. I read one of his poems in a magazine, and it was so impressive I wrote him a letter."

"Rhymed poetry?" Dr. Wood asked, with a wink at old Tick.

"Yes," said Warner. "I read all his manuscripts. They were sort of revolutionary. His poetry was a cry against injustice. Every kind of injustice. Bitter and burning."

"Wait a minute," Dr. Rosson said. "The new member seems to have some misconception of our function. We are not a literary society, Warner."

"And before you get started"—Dr. Hume grinned—"no bragging. You can do your bragging at the annual surgeons' convention."

"Gentlemen," Warner said, "I have no intention of bragging. I'll stick to murder, I assure you. And as bad a one as you've ever heard."

"Good," Dr. Kurtiff said. "Go on. And take it easy and don't break down."

"Yes." Dr. Wood grinned. "I remember when Morris here made his first confession. We had to pour a quart of whisky into him before he quit blubbering."

"I won't break down," Warner said. "Don't worry.

Well, the patient was sick for two weeks before I was called."

"I thought you were his friend," Dr. Davis said.

"I was," Warner answered. "But he didn't believe in doctors, so he did not consult one."

"No faith in them, eh?" Old Tick cackled. "Brilliant boy."

"He was," said Warner eagerly. "I felt upset when I came and saw how sick he was. I had him moved to a hospital at once."

"Oh, a rich poet," Dr. Sweeney said.

"No," said Warner. "I paid his expenses. And I spent all the time I could with him. The sickness had started with a severe pain on the left side of the abdomen. He was going to call me, but the pain subsided after three days, so the patient thought he was well. But it came back in two days, and he began running a temperature. He developed diarrhea. There was pus and blood, but no amoeba or pathogenic bacteria when he finally sent for me.

"After the pathology reports I made a diagnosis of ulcerative colitis. The pain being on the left side ruled out appendix. I put the patient on sulfaguanidine and unconcentrated liver extract, and gave him a high protein diet—chiefly milk. Despite this treatment and constant observation, the patient got worse. He developed generalized abdominal tenderness, both direct and rebound, and rigidity of the entire left rectus muscle. After two weeks of careful treatment, the patient died."

"And the autopsy showed you'd been wrong?" Dr.

Wood asked.

"I didn't make an autopsy," said Warner. "The boy's parents had perfect faith in me. As did the boy. They both believed I was doing everything possible to save his life."

"Then how do you know you were wrong in your diagnosis?" Dr. Hume asked.

"By the simple fact," said Warner irritably, "that the patient died instead of being cured. When he died I knew I had killed him by a faulty diagnosis."

"A logical conclusion," said Dr. Sweeney. "Pointless medication is no alibi."

"Well, gentlemen," old Tick said from behind his table, "our talented new member has obviously polished off a great poet and close personal friend. Indictments of his diagnosis are now in order."

But no one spoke. Doctors have a sense for things unseen and complications unstated. And nearly all the fourteen looking at Warner felt there was something hidden. The surgeon's tension, his elation and its overtone of mockery, convinced them there was something untold in the story of the dead poet. They approached the problem cautiously.

"How long ago did the patient die?" Dr. Rosson asked.

"Last Wednesday," said Warner. "Why?"

"What hospital?" asked Davis.

"St. Michael's," said Warner.

"You say the parents had faith in you," said Kurtiff, "and still have. Yet you seem curiously worried about something. Has there been any inquiry by the police?"

"No," said Warner. "I committed the perfect crime. The police haven't even heard of it. And even my victim died full of gratitude." He beamed at the room. "Listen," he went on, "even you people may not be able to disprove my diagnosis."

This brash challenge irritated a number of the members.

"I don't think it will be very difficult to knock out your diagnosis," said Dr. Morris.

"There's a catch to it," said Wood slowly, his eyes boring at Warner.

"The only catch there is," said Warner quickly, "is the complexity of the case. You gentlemen evidently prefer the simpler malpractice type of crime, such as I've listened to tonight."

There was a pause, and then Dr. Davis inquired in a soothing voice, "You described an acute onset of pain before the diarrhea, didn't you?"

"That's right," said Warner.

"Well," Davis continued coolly, "the temporary relief of symptoms and their recurrence within a few days sounds superficially like ulcers—excepting for one single point."

"I disagree," Dr. Sweeney said softly. "Dr. Warner's diagnosis is a piece of blundering stupidity. The symptoms he has presented have nothing to do with ulcerative colitis."

Warner flushed and his jaw muscles moved angrily. "Would you mind backing up your insults with a bit of science?" he said.

"Very easily done," Sweeney answered calmly. "The late onset of diarrhea and fever you describe rule out ulcerative colitis in ninety-nine cases out of a hundred. What do you think, Dr. Tick?"

"No ulcers," said Tick, his eyes studying Warner.

"You mentioned a general tenderness of the abdomen as one of the last symptoms," said Dr. Davis smoothly.

"That's right," said Warner.

"Well, if you have described the case accurately," Davis continued, "there is one obvious fact revealed. The general tenderness points to a peritonitis. I'm certain an autopsy would show that this perforation had walled off and spilled over and that a piece of intestine was telescoped into another."

"I don't think so," Dr. William Zinner, the cancer research man, said. He was short, bird-faced, and barely audible. Silence fell on the room, and the others waited attentively for his soft voice.

"It couldn't be an intussusception such as Dr. Davis describes," he went on. "The patient was only seventeen. Intussusception is unusual at that age unless the patient has a tumor of the intestines. In which case he would not have stayed alive that long."

"Excellent," old Tick spoke.

"I thought of intussusception," said Warner, "and discarded it for that very reason."

"How about a twisted gut?" Dr. Wood asked. "That could produce the symptoms described."

"No," said Dr. Rosson. "A volvulus means gangrene and death in three days. Warner says he attended his patient for two weeks and that the boy was sick for two weeks before Warner was called. The length of the illness rules out intussusception, volvulus, and intestinal tumor."

"There's one other thing," Dr. Morris said. "A left-sided appendix is a possibility, isn't it?"

"That's out, too," Dr. Wood said quickly. "The first symptom of a left-sided appendix would not be the acute pain described by Warner."

"The only thing we have determined," said Dr. Sweeney, "is a perforation other than ulcer. Why not go on with that?"

"Yes," said Dr. Morris. "Ulcerative colitis is out of the question considering the course taken by the disease. I'm sure we're dealing with another type of perforation."

"The next question," announced old Tick, "is what made the perforation?"

Dr. Warner mopped his face with his wet handkerchief and said softly, "I never thought of an object perforation."

"You should have," Dr. Kurtiff stated.

"Come, come," old Tick interrupted. "Let's not wander. What caused the perforation?"

"He was seventeen," Kurtiff answered, "and too old to be swallowing pins."

"Unless," said Dr. Hume, "he had a taste for pins. Did the patient want to live, Warner?"

"He wanted to live," said Warner grimly, "more than anybody I ever knew."

"I think we can ignore the suicide theory," said Dr. Kurtiff. "I am certain we are dealing with a perforation of the intestines and not of the subconscious."

"Well," Dr. Wood spoke, "it couldn't have been a chicken bone. A chicken bone would have stuck in the esophagus and never got through to the stomach."

"There you are, Warner," old Tick said. "We've narrowed it down. The spreading tenderness you described means a spreading infection. The course taken by the disease means a perforation other than ulcerous. And a perforation of that type means an object swallowed. We have ruled out pins and chicken bones. Which leaves us with only one other normal guess."

"A fishbone," said Dr. Sweeney.

"Exactly," said Tick.

Warner stood listening tensely to the voices affirming the diagnosis. Tick delivered the verdict.

"I think we are all agreed," he said, "that Sam Warner killed his patient by treating him for ulcerative colitis when an operation removing an abscessed fishbone would have saved his life."

Warner moved quickly across the room to the closet where he had hung his hat and coat.

"Where are you going?" Dr. Wood called after him. "We've just started the meeting."

Warner was putting on his coat and grinning.

"I haven't got much time," he said, "but I want to

thank all of you for your diagnosis. You were right about there being a catch to the case. The catch is that my patient is still alive. I've been treating him for ulcerative colitis for two weeks, and I realized this afternoon that I had wrongly diagnosed the case—and that he would be dead in twenty-four hours unless I could find out what really was the matter with him."

Warner was in the doorway, his eyes glittering.

"Thanks again, gentlemen, for the consultation and your diagnosis," he said. "It will enable me to save my patient's life."

A half-hour later, the members of the X Club stood grouped in one of the operating rooms of St. Michael's Hospital. They looked different from the men who had been playing a medical Halloween in the Walton Hotel. There is a change that comes over doctors when they face disease. The oldest and the weariest of them draws vigor from a crisis. The shambles leave them, and it is the straight back of the champion that enters the operating room. Confronting the problem of life and death, the tired, red-rimmed eyes become full of greatness and even beauty.

On the operating table lay the unconscious body of a Negro boy. Dr. Warner in his surgical whites stood over him.

The fourteen other X Club members watched Warner operate. Wood nodded approvingly at his speed. Rosson cleared his throat to say something, but the swift-moving hands of the surgeon held him silent. No one spoke. The minutes passed. The nurses quietly handed instruments to the surgeon. Blood spattered their hands and reddened the fronts of their white aprons.

Fourteen great medical men stared hopefully at the pinched and unconscious face of a colored boy who had swallowed a fishbone. No king or pope ever lay ill with more medical genius holding its breath around him.

Suddenly the perspiring surgeon raised something aloft in his forceps.

"Wash this off," he muttered to the nurse, "and show it to these gentlemen."

He busied himself placing drains in the abscessed cavity and then powdered some sulfanilamide into the opened abdomen to kill the infection.

Old Tick stepped forward and took the object from the nurse's hand.

"A fishbone," he said.

The X Club gathered around it as if it were a treasure indescribable.

"The removal of this small object," old Tick cackled softly, "will enable the patient to continue writing poetry denouncing the greeds and horrors of our world."

That, in effect, was the story Hume told me, plus the epilogue of the Negro poet's recovery three weeks later. We had long finished dinner and it was late night when we stepped into the war-dimmed streets of New York. The headlines on the newsstands had changed in size only. They were larger in honor of the larger slaughters they heralded.

Looking at them, you could see the death-strewn wastes of battles. But another picture came to my mind —a picture that had in it the hope of a better world. It was the hospital room in which *fifteen* famed and learned heroes stood battling for the life of a Negro boy who had swallowed a fishbone.

ERIC WILLIAMS

. . . was shot down over Germany in 1942, having flown with the R.A.F. since the outbreak of World War II in 1939. As a flight-lieutenant, he was imprisoned in Stalag Luft III—the same prison camp for Allied fliers from which Paul Brickhill helped engineer the greatest mass escape of the war.

This is the true account of Eric Williams' daring and ingenious prison break. Not since the first wooden horse was used by the Greeks in the Seige of Troy has so daring and audacious a scheme been carried off with such unbelievable success. To make his story more vivid, Williams tells it in the third person and refers to himself as Peter Howard—but every detail is authentic and every experience is one he, himself, endured.

From the moment Williams heard the gates of Stalag Luft III shut behind him, he dreamed of escape. Dozens of attempts had already been made to tunnel under the barbed-wire barriers. Highly trained dogs, seismographs, and the constantly searching guards had doomed these attempts to failure. But instead of tunneling from under the floor of the prison, he had the revolutionary idea of starting his tunnel out in the open within a few feet of the barrier—but also right under the noses of the patrolling sentries!

THE WOODEN HORSE

IT WAS JANUARY when they had first come to Stalag-Luft III, and for the whole of that month the ground was under snow. When the thaw came the camp was a sea of mud. But with the spring, came a renewed interest in escape. Spring is the escaping season. Peter and John had already escaped once from their previous camp, only to be brought back after two days of wandering aimlessly around the Polish countryside!

As the weather grew warmer they were ready to try again. For weeks now they had been talking of starting a tunnel. But all the possible starting places had been used before.

The camp was set in a clearing of the pine forest; a few single-story wooden barracks raised on piles three feet above the ground, huddled together inside the wire; strong and heavily interlaced, it was a twelve-foot double fence of bristling spikes. There were arc lamps hanging above the wire and at intervals along each fence stood "goon boxes," small sentry boxes on stilts higher than the wire. These were armed with machine-guns and carried searchlights which swept the dark continually. There were two guards in each box, connected by telephone to the main guardroom at the prison gates. Sentries carrying tommy-guns patrolled the wire between the sentry boxes.

Fifteen feet inside the main fence was a single strand of barbed wire twelve inches above the ground. This was the trip wire and anyone stepping over it was shot at by the guards. A narrow pathway trodden by the feet of the prisoners ran around the camp just inside the trip wire. This was their exercise ground, known as the circuit.

Under the gray dust of the compound the subsoil was clean hard yellow sand, which dried to a startling whiteness in the sun. The Germans knew that every tunnel carried its embarrassment of excavated sand and viewed each disturbance of this gray upper layer with suspicion. The skin of gray dust formed one of the most effective defenses of the camp.

Peter and John walked slowly, hands in pockets, round the circuit of the wire, idly watched by the sentries in the boxes. As they walked they were speaking in low tones.

"Pity about Bill's scheme," Peter said. "I thought they stood a chance with that."

"It was too far from the wire," John told him. "Think of all the sand you've got to hide to dig a tunnel three hundred feet long. The only way is to start somewhere out here, near the trip wire."

"You couldn't do it. There's nowhere near the wire to start a tunnel from."

"Why not start out in the open here—camouflage the trap?"

"But that's impossible. Every spot of ground near the trip wire is in full view of at least three goon boxes and two outside guards. Besides—how would you get the sand away?"

"It was done once. A crowd went out with a chap who played an accordion. While he played they all sat round in a big circle and sang. And while they were singing they dug a hole in the middle, passed the sand around and filled their pockets with it."

They walked on in silence. To Peter the idea was worth considering. "All we need is something to cover it with," he said. "Some sort of innocent activity like the accordion. But we can't do that again—must be known by now."

Peter looked over to the south where the tops of the trees were bending and waving. Then came sudden gusts of wind, catching at windows left loosely open, blowing up spouts of sand, snatching at the washing hung on lines outside the huts. Leaves and bits of paper were caught up and flung into the air. Far away a piece of newspaper was floating downwards and, as Peter watched, it drifted on to the tops of the pines, hung absurdly for a moment and then slipped out of sight.

Wish that was me, he thought. I could do with a miracle like that. Like old Elijah. Or the Greek tragedies. *Deus ex machina.* When the plot got stuck, you lowered a god down in a box and he sorted everything out. He pictured a genial old man with an olive wreath drifting down into the camp and offering him a lift. "Any more for the Skylark? Penny a ride on Pegasus. . . ."

An idea raced through his mind. The god in the box—the Trojan horse. "Pete!" he exploded. "What about the wooden horse of Troy?"

Peter laughed. "The wooden horse of Troy?"

"Yes, but a vaulting horse, a box horse like we had at school. We could carry it out every day and vault over it. One of us would be inside digging while the others vaulted."

"What about the sand we dig up?"

"We'll keep the horse in one of the huts and get the chaps to carry it out with one of us inside it. We'll take the sand back with us when we go in."

"It'll have to be a bloody strong horse."

"Oh, we'll manage it all right." John could see it already. As a complete thing. The wooden vaulting horse, the vertical shaft under it, and the long straight tunnel. He could see them working day after day until they got the tunnel dug. And he saw them going out through the tunnel.

"Let's go and see the Escape Committee now," he

said. "Someone else might think of it while we're still talking about it."

An hour later they were back walking the circuit. They had put the scheme before the Committee who were at first incredulous, then mocking, finally intrigued. They had registered the idea as their own and had been told that if they could produce the vaulting horse the scheme would have the full backing of the Committee.

"We'll have to get some strong pieces of wood for the framework," Peter said. "Then we've got to cover the sides."

"I was thinking of that. Why not cover them with canvas?"

Peter discarded the idea. "The sides will have to be solid otherwise there's no point in covering them at all. And if we do anything pointless the goons will get suspicious. No, this vaulting horse can't have anything phony about it."

"But do you realize what it'll weigh if we made the sides of solid wood? It would be as much as we could do to lift it, let alone carry someone inside it."

They walked on in silence, pacing slowly round the wire.

"I've got it, John!" Peter said suddenly, pointing to the unfinished washhouse. "We'll pinch some of the rafters out of the roof of the new shower baths. Get some nails too while we're about it."

"We'll have to do it after dark," John said. "There's no moon now, let's do it tonight."

From dusk until dawn the prisoners were locked in the huts while outside in the compound the darkness was stabbed and dissected by the searchlight beams which swept the camp continually throughout the night.

Peter had spent hours watching them. At times there seemed just time to dash quickly from one hut to another in the interval between the beams. Then, with startling abruptness, the beam would stab out in a totally unexpected quarter, utterly confounding the system.

It was eight twenty-five in the evening. Five minutes before zero hour. In Peter's room the men sat around the table talking nervously. There was an air of tension and an eagerness to get it over with.

During the afternoon Peter had loosened several boards in the floor. The huts stood on wooden piles raised a few feet above the level of the sand. Often during the night Peter had heard the dogs sniffing and prowling about under the floor.

He was frightened of them. There was something terrifying to him in the thought of the dogs prowling about in the darkness. Animals trained by men to hunt men! Where would the dogs stop if they caught you? He glanced impatiently at his watch.

John sat, a mirror in front of him, smearing wood-ash on his face to blacken it. "What time is it, Pete?"

"Twenty twenty-five. Better wait until twenty-thirty before we go. I hope Tony doesn't bungle things at the other end."

"What's he going to do?"

John was still rubbing wood-ash on his face. "He's going to crawl out of the bottom hut to attract the dogs up to that end of the camp." He looked again at his watch. "O.K., John. Off we go!"

They lowered themselves through the trapdoor into the darkness under the hut. It took them some time to crawl through the wire surrounding the shower house.

Once inside, with the wire replaced, they were free from the dogs and searchlights and could work in peace. They worked fast. There were some long wooden rafters lying against one of the walls and these Peter sawed into suitable lengths with a small hacksaw blade. John searched for nails and any odd tools lying around, which he quickly stuffed into his pockets.

When Peter had collected sufficient timber he passed it to John who had crawled back through the wire, and between them they dragged it to the hut.

Several times on the way back they had to lie flat while a searchlight enveloped them in its blinding light. It's just like flying over Berlin, Peter thought. Just the same feeling of naked vulnerability.

There was more than the usual noise coming from the hut that night from their fellow prisoners. A carefully orchestrated background to drown the sound of their working. Peter knew that every blackout shutter in the hut was unfastened, that men were waiting in every room to drag them inside should they have to bolt for it.

They gained the hut without being discovered and buried the timber and the tools in the sand under it.

The next morning Peter went along to the Wing Commander's room to borrow some tools, while John canvassed the compound for prisoners who were willing to vault.

The wing commander had a remarkable collection of tools.

"It's a wonder the goons don't take your tools away," Peter remarked.

The wing commander looked cunning. "Look at this." He pointed to a tool rack fixed to the wall over the workbench. "Have a look at these tools."

Peter examined the tools. Every one was phony. It must have taken "Wings" weeks to fashion the hacksaw blades and wicked-looking knives from pieces of rolled-out tin cans. There were chisels too, made of wood and painted to look like steel.

"They do a swoop now and again, but all they find is this. All my real tools are hidden behind the paneling of the wall. They think I'm mad, but quite harmless, really."

Peter laughed. "I expect they think most of us are looney. I want to make a vaulting horse and I came along to ask your advice and see if you could let me have a bit of plywood and some nails."

"Yes, I think so." To him a vaulting horse was a problem in terms of materials available.

Peter explained about the tunnel. He did not want the wing commander to be working in the dark.

"Wings" was at once enthusiastic.

"We must set it out first," he said. He pinned up a sheet of clean paper on his drawing board. "It will have to be light and strong," he said. "Strong both ways. Both for vaulting and for carrying you inside it." He took up a scale rule and bent over the board.

Between them they had built the vaulting horse. It stood four feet six inches high, the base covering an area of five feet by three feet. The sides were covered with two-feet square plywood sheets from Red Cross packing cases stolen from the German store. The sides tapered up to the top which was of solid wood boards padded with their bedding and covered with white linen material taken from the bales in which the cigarettes arrived from England.

There were four slots cut in the plywood sides. When pieces of rafter had been pushed through these holes the horse could be carried by four men in the manner of a sedan chair.

Some days after John had recruited prisoners for vaulting, the few afternoon walkers on the circuit were surprised to see the double doors of the canteen open and a team of prisoners dressed only in shorts march down the wooden steps and form up in a line near the trip wire. They were followed by the four strongest members of the team who carried a boxlike object slung on wooden poles to a spot about thirty feet inside the trip wire where it was carefully placed on the ground and the poles withdrawn.

The team formed up and under the direction of one of the prisoners began to vault over the box. The guards turned toward the unusual spectacle. The standard of vaulting was high. But one of the men's approach was clumsy and his vaulting not up to the standard of the others. The guards grinned whenever he failed to clear the horse. Every time he failed to clear it he drew jeers and catcalls from the surrounding prisoners.

Soon the guards in the boxes were leaning on their elbows waiting for him to make his run. He took a final, desperate leap and in missing his footing he lurched into the horse and knocked it over. He knocked it over on to its side so that the interior was in full view of the guards.

The horse was empty. The vaulters righted the box and went on with their sport. Soon they carried the horse back into the canteen, where they left it until the following afternoon.

Before they left the canteen they tied pieces of black thread across the doorway and from the edge of the horse to the skirting board. The following morning the thread was broken. The ferrets were taking no chances. (The special security guards were called ferrets by the prisoners.) During the night the vaulting horse had been examined.

A week after the vaulting had first started, Peter and John were walking round the circuit. The subject of their conversation—it had been nothing else for a week—was the vaulting horse.

"I think we might start digging tomorrow," John said. "The goons have got used to the vaulting now. We've knocked the horse over often enough for them to see that there's nothing going on inside. How long do you think it'll take us to dig the tunnel?"

"Let's see." John hitched his shorts with his elbows. "We've got about forty-five feet to go to the trip wire, thirty feet across the danger strip. The wire itself is about eight feet thick so that makes eighty-three feet. We should break at least thirty feet beyond the wire because of the outside sentries. That gives us one hundred and thirteen feet altogether. Allow a bit for going round rock or tree roots and make it a round figure of one hundred and twenty feet . . . if we do five feet a day it will take us twenty-four days."

"It's not a matter of how much we can dig in a day—it's a matter of how much we can carry away in the horse—with one of us inside as well."

"Supposing we say we can carry about a hundred and forty pounds of sand and another hundred and fifty for one of us—I think a foot a day seems more reasonable than three feet."

That evening Peter made the top section of the shoring for the vertical shaft. He made it with four sides of a plywood packing case reinforced and slotted so that they could be assembled into a rigid four-sided box without top or bottom. The box would stand considerable inward pressure.

John spent the evening in making twelve bags

from the bottoms of trouser legs. Several of the prisoners had made themselves shorts by cutting their trousers off above the knee. When John had sewn the bottoms together, roughly hemmed the tops and inserted string, the trouser legs had become bags about twelve inches long. He fashioned hooks from strong wire with which he intended to suspend the bags inside the horse.

During the week they had made two sand pits, one at the side and one at the head of where the horse was standing. They had made these ostensibly to soften the shock of landing on their bare feet. Actually they served as a datum mark to ensure that they always replaced the horse on the exact spot.

The next afternoon they took the horse out with John inside it. He took with him a cardboard Red Cross box to hold the surface sand, the trouser-leg bags and hooks, one side of the vertical shoring, and a bricklayer's trowel they had stolen from the unfinished shower baths.

Inside the horse, his feet were on the bottom framework, one on each side. In his arms he held the equipment. The horse creaked and lurched as the bearers staggered under the unaccustomed weight. They got the horse into position and began to vault.

John worked quickly inside. Scraping up the dark gray surface sand, he put it into the cardboard box and started to dig a deep trench for one side of the shoring. He put the bright yellow excavated sand into the trouser-leg bags.

As the trench grew deeper he had difficulty in reaching the bottom. He made it wider and had to bank the extra sand against one end of the horse. It was hot inside and he began to sweat.

He finished the trench and put the plywood sheet in position. He replaced the surplus sand, ramming it down with the handle of the trowel, packing the shoring tight. The top of the shoring was six inches below the ground.

Standing on the framework of the horse, he carefully spread the sand over the plywood sheet, packing it down hard, finally sprinkling the gray sand over the whole area covered by the horse—obliterating any foot and finger marks he thought would show.

Calling softly to Peter, he gave the word that he had finished.

The vaulters inserted the carrying poles and staggered back into the canteen with John and the bags of sand.

Once inside the canteen they transferred the sand from the trouser-leg bags into long, sausagelike sacks made from the arms and legs of woolen underwear. These they carried away slung around their necks and down inside their trouser-legs.

The sand was dispersed in various places around the compound, some of it finding its way by devious routes to the latrines, some of it buried under the huts, some of it carried out in specially made trouser pockets and dug into the tomato patches outside the huts.

It took them four days to sink the four sides of the box. Working alternately, they sank the box in the ground and removed the sand from inside it. When they reached the bottom of the woodwork they dug deeper still, putting bricks under the four corners of the box to support it. They made a trap of bed-boards and replaced this and the surface sand whenever they left the hole.

Finally they had made a hole five feet deep and two feet six inches square. They had dropped the wooden box twelve inches as they worked. The top of the box was now eighteen inches below the surface of the ground. They filled bags, made from woolen undervests, and placed them on top of the trap, covering them with merely six to eight inches of surface sand. The bags were thin enough not to impede the progress of the guards' probing rods and deadened any hollow sound if the trap were walked on.

The wooden box stood on four brick piles two feet high. On three sides the shaft below the wooden box was shored with pieces of bed-board. The fourth side was left open for the tunnel.

It was possible to stand in the shaft, but it was not possible to kneel. To get into the tunnel they were forced to make a short burrow in the opposite direction. Into this they thrust their feet while kneeling to enter the tunnel.

The first seven feet of the tunnel was shored solid with bed-boards to take the impact of the vaulters on the surface. The shoring was made by Peter, in the evenings, in the security of their room and taken down to the tunnel in sections and reassembled there. The whole of the work was done with a table knife and a red-hot poker.

To assemble the shoring Peter lay on his back in the darkness of the narrow tunnel, scraping away sufficient sand to slide the main bearers into position before inserting the bed-boards. He had to work slowly and carefully, fearful all the time that a sudden fall of sand would bury him. Even a small fall would be enough to pin him, helpless, on his back in the narrowness of the tunnel.

When the ceiling of the tunnel was in position they had to fill the space between the top of the tunnel and the wooden ceiling with sand. If this were not done the sand would fall and the ceiling become higher and higher until a telltale subsidence of the surface would reveal the path of the tunnel.

While one of them supervised the vaulting the other dug in the tunnel. It was fingers and toes all the way until he got to the end of the tunnel. Once he got there he scraped some sand from the face with a trowel and crawled backward down the tunnel, dragging the sand with him. When he got back to the vertical shaft he had brought enough sand to fill half a bag. And there were twelve bags to fill.

There was no light in the tunnel and very little air. He spent his spell of work in a bath of perspiration— even the lightest clothes scraped a certain amount of sand from the sides of the tunnel as he crawled along.

Each bag of sand that was scraped from the sides of the tunnel meant one less bag taken from the face. So he worked entirely naked and as he sweated the sand caked on him. He got sand in his eyes, in his ears, in his nose, and all over his head. As the tunnel grew longer the work became more difficult and the air more foul. They did not put up air holes for fear the dogs would sniff them through the openings.

Not only were the tunnellers exhausted by the twenty-four times repeated crawl up the tunnel, but the vaulters—who had been vaulting every afternoon of the two months that it had taken to dig forty feet —were exhausted too. The tunnellers were given extra food, but the vaulters were not, and they had little energy to spare.

A dozen men could not vault for two hours without looking unnatural about it. The whole time one of the tunnellers was below ground the other would be in the vaulting team trying to make the two hours that the horse stood there appear as natural as possible. It was not easy, especially when the ferret was standing within earshot of the horse, watching the vaulting.

They organized a medicine-ball and deck-tennis quoit and stood in a circle around the horse throwing them to one another. They even organized a run around the circuit—leaving the horse vulnerable and alone with the trap open below it.

The end came one afternoon while John was in the tunnel. Peter had gone to the main gate to find out how many Germans were in the compound. It was ten minutes before they were due to take the horse in. As he was walking back toward the horse he was met by one of the vaulters, pale-faced and running.

"What's wrong?" Peter asked.

"There's been a fall near the horse."

"Is John all right?"

"We shouted to him, but we can't get a reply."

Peter ran toward the horse. John would be caught in the end of the tunnel, suffocating, trapped by the fall of sand!

The vaulters were grouped around a man who was lying on the ground. Peter glanced quickly toward the sentry boxes above the wire. The guards were watching.

"Where's the fall?" he asked.

"Nigel's lying on it. A hole suddenly appeared, so Nigel lay across it. He's pretending he's hurt his leg. We can't get a reply from John."

Oh God, Peter thought, John's had it. He wanted to overturn the horse and go down, but old John would be furious if he panicked for nothing, and the tunnel was discovered.

"Send someone for a stretcher," he said. "We must make this look as natural as possible."

Peter crouched by Nigel's feet, his head near the horse. "John," he called. "John!" No answer.

"Roll over, Nig," he said.

Nigel rolled over. There was a hole, about as thick as his arm, going down into the darkness of the tunnel.

"John," he called. "John!"

"Hallo, Pete." The answer was weak. "I can clear it. I've taken some of the shoring from the shaft. Can you fill it from the top?"

"O.K. Let me know when you've got it fixed." He pretended to attend to Nigel's leg. "The chaps with the stretcher will be here in a minute," Peter told him. "They'll carry you to your hut. That'll explain what we've been doing."

Presently he heard John's voice, thinly, from inside the tunnel. "I'm just putting the shoring in. You can fill-in in about five minutes."

What a man, Peter thought. What a man! Good old John. He poked solicitously at Nigel's leg. The two vaulters returned with the stretcher and a first-aid kit. Peter made a great business of bandaging Nigel's leg while the others, shuffling around, kicked the sand toward the hole.

Ten minutes passed. Still there was no sign from John.

If we can't get him up before roll call we've had it, Peter thought. "Come on, chaps," he said. "We can't just stand around here."

They began to vault again. Then he heard John's voice, urgently, from inside the horse. "Hey, Pete, what's the time?"

"You've got five minutes before roll call."

"It's an awful mess."

At the end of the five minutes they carried him into the canteen. He could hardly stand. "It's a terrible mess," he said. "There's a bit of tree root there and the vaulting must have shaken it loose. I've jammed it up temporarily but it needs proper shoring."

The next afternoon Peter went down with some wooden shoring. He found the tunnel choked with sand that continued to fall as he worked. He worked entirely by feel, and the air was bad so that he panted as he worked. Sand fell into his eyes and his mouth. He worked furiously, clearing the sand away and fitting the shoring into position.

When he finally got back into the horse he could hardly find the strength to replace the trap. He put it back, and the sand above it, and gave John the signal that he was ready to be taken in. When he reached the canteen he crawled out from under the horse and fainted.

That evening he was taken to the camp hospital. It was a total collapse. He had taken too much out of himself with the digging, the vaulting, and the worry. The British doctor prescribed a week in bed.

During the week he was in the hospital no digging was done; but the horse was taken out every afternoon to avoid the suspicion of the guards.

Peter used this period of enforced idleness to cultivate Dopey, one of the hospital guards. He was a simple man, a man of small loyalties. For a bar of chocolate he would forget his obligation to the Third

Reich. For a cigarette he would agree that the Allies would probably win the war.

One day when Dopey came in for his cup of cocoa Peter talked to him. After much questioning and cigarette bribes, Peter discovered that the railways were overcrowded, trains were running late and, above all, that foreign workers were allowed to travel on the trains. But they had to have special passes.

From then on Peter cultivated Dopey in every way. He gave him cigarettes and cocoa and when the time was ripe he asked Dopey to borrow one of the foreign workers' passes and bring it into the camp for him to see. Dopey refused. He was terrified. Nothing would make him budge.

Peter played his trump card. "You have been trading with the prisoners. I have three witnesses. If you do not bring me the passes I shall report you to the Camp Kommandant. We shall go to the cooler. But you—you will be shot."

Dopey whined and pleaded, but he was caught and he knew it. The next morning he brought the passes. Peter made a careful copy of them and returned them to Dopey the same evening. The passes would have to be forged properly when he got back to the camp; but he knew what they were like. He was equipped now and he bided his time. During the long hours of idleness in the hospital he had completed his plans for the journey to neutral territory. He waited impatiently to get back to the tunnel.

When Peter came out of the hospital he and John discussed the tunnel. As usual they discussed it while walking around the circuit, the only place in the compound safe from the ears of the ferrets.

"It's quite obvious," Peter was saying, "that we can't go on as we are. We're taking two hours to dig out twelve bags and it'll take about half an hour to crawl up to the face once we get to a hundred feet. It's not like wriggling on the surface." He waited.

"There's always a way," John said. "Let's study the problem. It's how to get the sand from the face to the shaft."

Peter grunted and they walked on in silence. There must be some way, he thought, of getting the sand out of the place. . . .

Then he saw it. "I've got an idea," he said. "We'll go down together. The chaps should be able to carry us. Then we'll have to make thirty-six bags instead of the original twelve. And we'll have to make a small chamber at the end of the tunnel to give us room to work. We'll run a toboggan between us with a rope at each end. One will work in the chamber and the other in the vertical shaft. When we've filled the thirty-six bags we'll stack them all in the shaft and go back in the horse without any sand."

"You mean, leave all the thirty-six bags in the tunnel?"

"I'm coming to that. We do that in the afternoon. The same evening one of us goes out alone in the horse and brings back twelve of the bags. The next

afternoon the other brings back twelve more, and the
last twelve that evening. The next afternoon we both
go out and dig another thirty-six."

"We shan't average more than six inches a day,"
John said.

"We'll have to revise our ideas, that's all; and we'll
have to bring someone else in to organize the vaulting. We can't both be underground without having
someone up there's who's in the scheme."

"I thought just we two were going to be in it. I
thought we were going to keep it small."

"Yes, but we've got to adapt our plans as we go
along. It's too much to ask a chap to organize all the
vaulting and not give him a chance to go out with
us. What about Philip?"

"O.K." John said, "let's go and find him."

They ran him to earth near the gate leading to the
Vorlager.

"You're mad," Philip said. "You're both mad. Leave
me alone—and find someone else to pester."

"We mean it, Phil," John said. "We want you to
join us in the job."

Philip finally agreed very reluctantly. "I'll come in.
But I don't think we've a hope of ever getting out."

"You stick by us," John assured him. "You'll get
out."

A newly arrived prisoner on his first visit to the
barber's shop was astounded to see the door open and
a naked, brown, tousle-headed, sand and sweat-stained

figure crawl in on all fours carrying with him a khaki-colored bag tied at the neck with string.

Without saying a word, ignored by the barber and his waiting clients, the strange figure crawled to the window, opened a trap in the floor and disappeared from view, dragging the bag after him. Then another fully-dressed figure appeared with another bag, followed by others who formed a human chain, passing the bags from hand to hand down to the naked one under the floor.

Suddenly, a vacant-eyed violinist standing by the window stopped playing a low, sad melody. The trap was closed immediately on the man under the floor and the human chain became an orchestra earnestly playing the various musical instruments which had been lying close at hand.

A few minutes later one of the ferrets sauntered past the window. He did not look in. He would have seen only a prisoner having his hair cut, the waiting clients and the camp orchestra practicing in one corner of the room.

There was a loud knock on the door. The orchestra laid down their instruments and opened the trap. The violinist resumed his melancholy tune. Twelve empty bags were handed up from the hole in the floor and the naked one emerged. He was handed his clothes in silence and in silence he put them on. The trap was replaced, the empty bags were collected and one of the vaulters carefully swept the floor with his handkerchief to remove the last traces of sand.

After some months of work in the tunnel the space below the floor of the barber's shop was filled. The bags of sand were then carried out by the camp glee-singers, who rehearsed in the next room. The full bags were passed up through a trapdoor in the ceiling to Nigel, who spread the sand evenly between the joists in the beaverboard ceiling. They could not put much sand in the roof as the weight threatened to bring down the ceiling; so after a time another trapdoor was made over the kitchen.

It was now early October. All through the summer their working had been controlled by the weather. Once the trap was lifted and the workers were in the tunnel it took them all of fifteen minutes to get back to the shaft, close the trap and get ready to be carried in. They could not afford to be caught out by a shower of rain for the vaulters could not continue without arousing the suspicion of the guards. Nor could they run for the shelter of the canteen leaving the vaulting horse to stand out in the rain.

The obvious thing was to carry the horse in with them, and they could not do this with the trap open and two men in the tunnel. So they studied the weather carefully and if it looked at all like rain they had to vault without digging. Nearly every time they took the horse out it was only after long discussions on the weather. The nearer they got to the wire the more reluctant they were to risk being caught by the rain.

They were also determined to be out by the end of October and as the time passed they began to get dog-

matic and short-tempered in their discussions. It was
trying for all of them. They were physically tired after
three and a half months of digging and now their
nerves were becoming frayed by continual anxiety and
changes of plan.

With the new system of digging the tunnel made
slow progress. They had enlarged the end of the tunnel to form a bulge large enough to allow the man
working at the face to rest on his elbows and draw his
knees up under his chest. Instead of using the usual
wooden toboggan for carrying the sand down the tunnel they used a metal basin eighteen inches in diameter
and eight inches deep.

When the bulge was finished—it took them four
days to remove the extra sand—the tunnel was driven
on. One man worked in the tunnel extension, dragging
the sand backward into the bulge. Once in the bulge
he pulled the basin up the tunnel, past his feet and
over his legs on to his stomach, where he filled it with
the sand he had brought back. Two pulls on the rope
was the signal for the man in the shaft to pull back
the basin full of sand. He then tipped the basin over
and filled his bags while the worker in the bulge
crawled up the tunnel extension for more sand.

At first they merely threaded rope through two
holes they had made in the rim of the basin. But the
holes cut the string, leaving the basin stranded—usually
half-way up the tunnel. Then there followed a whispered argument as to who was nearer the basin and
whose turn it was to crawl up the tunnel and repair

the string. Later they made strong wire hooks with which to attach the basin to the rope.

They found that sufficient air was pushed up the tunnel by the passage of the basin to supply the man in the bulge. If for any reason the basin was not kept moving the shortage of air became dangerous.

After a time they drove the new tunnel so far beyond the bulge that it became impossible to work in the extension and they made a new bulge at the end of the tunnel, filled in the old bulge, lengthened the rope and carried on as before. They made three such bulges before the tunnel was complete.

It was a feat of some endurance to drag the thirty-odd full basins of sand from the face to the shaft. In addition to this the bags had to be filled and lifted one by one and stacked inside the vaulting horse.

When they had been digging for some months John became convinced that the tunnel was veering to the left. Peter crawled to the end of the tunnel with the rope of the basin tied to his ankle. He took with him a thin metal poker about four feet long.

John sat in the shaft holding the other end of the rope while Nigel sat on the horse apparently resting after an energetic bout of vaulting. Philip stood gazing vacantly out through the wire.

Peter, lying full length at the end of the tunnel, forced the poker upward through the tunnel's roof using a corkscrew motion to avoid bringing down the roof. Inch by inch he forced it upwards until by the sudden lack of resistance he knew that it was through and protruding above the surface of the ground. He gave two tugs on the rope to tell John that he was through. John knocked on the inside of the horse and Nigel, hearing this, sent a messenger across to Philip.

Philip, without appearing to do so, frantically scanned the ground in front of him for the end of the poker. When he saw it, he scratched his head. Nigel kicked the side of the horse. John pulled the rope. Peter pulled down the poker.

The end of the tunnel was fifteen feet to the left of where Peter had expected it to be.

The following morning Peter, John and Philip walked together round the wire completing their plans for the break.

"We're under the wire now and we've twelve days to go to the end of the month." Peter said. "If we're lucky we shall do another six feet by then. That puts us about three feet outside the wire. There's a shallow ditch about twelve feet beyond the wire and if we can manage to strike that it will give us some cover for the break."

"It's still in the light of the arc lamps," John objected.

"The light from the lamps extends for about thirty feet outside the wire and we can't possibly push the tunnel on as far as that. Besides, the only railway time-table we've got expires at the end of the month and we *must* time the break so that we just have time to leap down to the station and catch a train. If we get out and then have to hang about waiting for a train we stand a good chance of getting picked up right away."

"I agree with Pete," Philip said. "We'll just have to organize a diversion in the huts nearest the wire at the time that we mean to break."

"That won't be too easy," John said. "Who's going to estimate how long it's going to take us to mole the last ten feet?"

"We'll have to overestimate it," Peter said. "Then add half as much time again and if we reach the ditch before the time we've said—we'll just have to wait until we hear the diversion start." He turned to Philip. "Will you organize the diversion?"

"O.K. I'll get that fixed up. What about the outside sentries?"

"They don't come on until an hour after dusk. John and I have been sitting up all night watching them. There are two on the side where we are. They each patrol half the wire, meet in the middle, turn back to back and walk to the end. When the diversion starts they and the goons in the boxes will be looking in toward the noise. We should get past them all right." He spoke confidently, but thought of tommy-gun bullets and the sharp cry in the night when another escaping prisoner had been shot on the wire. "We shall have to wear dark clothes," he said.

"I'd thought of that," Philip said. "We've just had some long woolen underwear sent in by the Red Cross. If we dye them black with tea leaves or coffee grains we could put them on over our clothes. It will keep us clean while we're down there and be good camouflage when we get out."

"And we could wear socks over our shoes and black hoods over our heads," John added.

"We haven't solved the most important problem yet," Peter said. "How to get four people out in the horse."

"Four people?" Philip sounded excited. "I thought only we three were going!"

"Yes, but somebody's got to close the trap down after us."

Philip nearly choked. "D'you mean to say that you've got as far as this and never considered how we were to get out?"

"Did *you* consider it?" Peter asked.

"I thought you'd got it all fixed."

"We'll have to put the kit down the day before," John said.

"We can't do that," Peter said. "If we put three kitbags in the tunnel we shan't be able to get down ourselves."

"If I go down in the afternoon before roll call," John said, "and take the baggage with me, you can seal me down and I'll dig the whole of the afternoon. You can cook my absence at roll call and then you two come down as soon as you can. Take the smallest man we can find with you to seal the trap down after you, and then we'll have two hours in which to get ready to break."

"It'll be pretty grim," Peter said, "stuck down there

alone for a couple of hours."

"Oh, I shall be all right. I'll put an air hole up inside the wire and do five or six feet before you come down."

Peter knew John's unsparing energy once he'd set his heart to a thing. He was all energy once he started. Nervous energy and guts. "Remember we may have to run for it," he said. "Don't wear yourself out digging—leave most of it for when we get down there."

"Oh, I'll take it easy," John lied. Peter knew he lied and could do nothing about it.

For the next twelve days they vaulted every day and they increased the number of bags to fourteen and finally fifteen, although the extra load made the bearers stagger as they carried the horse into the canteen.

On October the twenty-eighth they made the final bulge at the end of the tunnel to hold their kitbags while they were digging the last ten feet and finally breaking through to the surface.

They spent the next morning bringing in the last twelve bags and recovering their civilian clothing from their various scattered hiding places round the camp. At twelve-thirty John had his last meal, a substantial meal of bully beef, potatoes, biscuits and cheese. He wore his civilian clothes under a long khaki Polish greatcoat. Earlier in the day their baggage had been taken to the canteen, hidden in bundles of dirty laundry.

"O.K.," said Peter. "Let's go!"

John hurriedly doffed his coat and pulled the long black underwear over his clothes. He pulled black socks over his shoes and adjusted the hood which was made from an old undervest dyed black. "It's bloody hot in here," he said.

They both crawled under the vaulting horse, Peter holding a blanket, a cardboard box, and twelve empty bags; John sinister in his black clothes. The three kit-bags hung between them suspended from the top of the horse. They both crouched with their backs to the ends of the horse, their feet one each side on the bottom framework. Then the bearing poles were inserted and the horse was raised and they went creaking across the compound toward the vaulting pits.

With a sigh of relief the bearers placed the horse in position and withdrew the poles ready for vaulting.

While John crawled up the tunnel Peter detached the metal basin from the end of the rope and tied one of the kitbags in its place. One by one John pulled the kitbags up the tunnel and put them in the bulge at the end. Peter then replaced the basin and between them they filled the twelve empty bags they had taken out with them.

While Peter was stacking the bags in the body of the horse, John crawled back for his last breath of fresh air. Outside they could hear the shouting of the vaulters and the reverberating concussion as they landed on top of the horse. John straightened up, head and shoulders out of the trap. He had left the hood at the end of the tunnel and his face was red.

"It's bloody hot down there with clothes on."

"Take it easy," Peter said. "For heaven's sake don't overdo it."

He watched John's legs disappear down the narrow tunnel; then he replaced the trap and the heavy bags of sand and stamped the loose sand firmly on top of them. It's burying a man alive, he thought. Then he heard an anxious voice from outside.

"How's it going, Pete?"

"Five minutes, Phil," he said, and started to hang the twelve bags of sand from the top of the horse. He gathered the blanket in his arms and spread the rest of the sand evenly over the ground under the horse. He sprinkled the dry gray sand from the cardboard box over this and gave Philip a low hail that he was ready.

As they neared the canteen he could hear the voices of the choir. "He shall set His angels guard over thee . . . Lest thou catch thy foot against a stone. . . ." He grinned widely in the dark belly of the horse.

With a final creaking lurch they were up the steps and inside the canteen. The old horse is falling to pieces, Peter thought. Hope it lasts out this evening.

Roll call was at 3:45 P.M. and Peter and Philip spent the time until then lying on their bunks. For Peter this was the worst moment of all. This waiting after the work had been done. This lying on his bunk while John was down below digging, and at any moment the scheme might blow and their four and a half months' effort be wasted.

Once they were outside he felt it wouldn't matter so much. He hardly expected to get back to England. That was looking too far ahead. That was too much in the lap of the gods. Anything might happen once they were outside. From the moment they left the end of the tunnel they would have to adapt their policy to the conditions they met. He could not plan ahead a single day.

And so he lay on his back on the bunk and let his mind run over the list of things he was taking with him.

There was the "dog food," a hard cake made from dried milk, sugar, Bemax, and cocoa. It had been packed in small square tins from the Red Cross parcels and he intended to wear a girdle of them between two shirts.

Next there were several linen bags containing a dry mixture of oatmeal, raisins, sugar, and milk powder. When they ate this it would swell in the stomach and prevent that hollow aching sickness that comes from eating ill-balanced concentrated food. He had sewn one of these bags into each armpit of his jacket as an emergency ration if he became separated from the attaché case which held the bulk of their food.

The attaché case was already down in the tunnel, at the bottom of the kitbag. He mentally checked its contents: the food, clean socks, shaving gear, a roll-neck sweater, soap, pen and ink for minor alterations to their papers, and spare cigarettes and matches.

He got to his feet and checked over his jacket

pockets. The wallet which held his papers and German money, a small pocket compass, a penknife, handkerchiefs, his pipe (a German one bought in the town by one of the guards), a length of string, a pencil, a German tobacco pouch, his beret, and a comb.

He went out on the circuit. It was no use, he couldn't be still. He walked around, over the tunnel, and thought of John moling away down there, sweating away, not knowing the time, not knowing whether the tunnel had been discovered, out of touch with everyone. John digging away, trying to get as much done as he could before the others joined him.

He then walked with Nigel several times round the circuit while they waited for roll call.

"I shall miss you after you've gone," Nigel said. "It's been quite good fun, this vaulting."

"I expect they'll take the horse away when they discover the tunnel," Peter said. He wanted to thank Nigel for all the help he had given, but he knew that he could not do it. To thank him would put the thing on a formal basis and it was beyond that. So they walked, trying to talk naturally, and waited for the roll call.

At roll call the Senior British Officer, suitably disguised, took John's place in the ranks and his absence was not noticed.

As soon as roll call was finished the vaulters assembled at the canteen. Peter's knees felt loose and he did not want to go in the horse. It was the first time they had vaulted after evening roll call and he was certain that the guards would be suspicious. As he pulled on the evil-smelling black- underwear he could hear Nigel instructing the four men who were to carry the horse. He looked at Philip, unrecognizable in his black hood; and then at the third man, McKay, who they had chosen as the lightest man in the camp.

Nigel came in and handed him a bottle of cold tea for John. "Give him my love," he said, "and tell him to write," he said nervously and added a wry smile.

Peter and Philip crawled under the horse, stood one at each end and held McKay suspended between them. The poles were placed in position; the horse protestingly started on its last journey and they went swaying and jerking across the football field.

Once the horse was in position Philip sat on McKay's back at one end while Peter again removed the trap. As he took out the wooden boards he listened for sounds of movement in the tunnel. It was silent. He looked at Philip.

"I'll go up the tunnel and see how John is," he said. "You fill twelve bags from the bottom of the shaft for Mac to take back, and then stay down this end. I'll send the sand back to you in the basin and you spread it along the floor of the tunnel as you come up."

"Right."

"You'll never get down there!" McKay looked with wonder at the narrowness of the shaft.

Peter dropped feet first into the vertical shaft and squirmed inch by inch along the hundred feet that had taken them so long to build. Now that it was finished he was almost sorry. The tunnel had been first in his thoughts for months, cherished, nursed; and now he was crawling down it for the last time.

As he neared the end of the tunnel he flashed the torch ahead and called softly to John. He was afraid to call loudly for he was now under the wire and close to the sentry's beat. He passed the bend where they had altered course and came to the end of the tunnel and a solid wall of sand.

John must have been digging steadily on and in banking up the sand behind him had completely blocked the tunnel.

Peter bored a small hole through the wall which was about three feet thick. As he broke through a gust of hot fetid air gushed out and there was John, wringing wet with perspiration and black from head to foot with the dye that had run out of his combinations.

"Where the blazes have you been?" he asked.

"It's only just about four-thirty," Peter said.

"I thought it was after six and that roll call had gone wrong and I'd have to go out alone."

"It's all O.K.," Peter said. "I've got a bottle of tea here." He pushed it through the hole to John. "I'll just send this sand back to Phil and then I'll join you." He pulled the empty basin up the tunnel and sent the first load back to Philip, who filled the empty bags he had brought down and stacked them in the shaft.

They worked feverishly trying to get as much as possible done before the breaking time. John, in front, stabbing at the face with a trowel and pushing the damp sand under his belly back toward Peter, who lay with his head on John's heels collecting the sand and squirming backward with it to Philip, who banked it up as a solid wall behind them. They were now in a narrow portion of the tunnel about twenty-five feet long and two feet square, ventilated by one small hole three inches in diameter.

They were working for the first time in clothes and for the first time without the fresh air pushed up the tunnel by the basin. They were working three in the tunnel and they were anxious about the air. The other prisoners had been locked in the huts for the night and if the tunnel collapsed now they were helpless.

They all worked fast and steadily. None of them wanted to be the one to break the rhythm of the work.

At five-thirty Peter, who had a watch, called a halt. "We'd better push up to the top now," he whispered. "We've got to be out in half an hour."

It was farther than they had expected and they thought they would never get to the top. Finally John broke through—a hole as large as his fist—and through it he caught his first glimpse of the stars. The stars in the free heavens beyond the wire!

"I'll break out the whole width of the tunnel," John whispered, "just leaving the thin crust over the top. Then we can break that quickly and there'll be less chance of being seen."

At exactly six o'clock they broke through to the open air, pulling the dry sandy surface down on top of them, choking and blinding them and making them want to cough. As they broke through they heard the sound of the diversion coming from the huts nearest the wire. There were men blowing trumpets, men singing, men banging the sides of the hut and yelling at the top of their voices.

"The silly idiots will get a bullet in there if they're not careful," John whispered.

"Go on! Go now!" Peter said. He was scared. It was too light.

Quickly John hoisted his kitbag out of the tunnel and rolled it toward the ditch. He squeezed himself out of the hole and Peter saw his legs disappear from view.

Peter stuck his head out of the tunnel and looked toward the camp. It was brilliantly floodlit. He had not realized how brilliantly it was lit. But the raised sentry boxes were in darkness and he could not see whether the guards were looking in his direction or not. He could not see the guards outside the wire.

He lifted out his kitbag and pushed it toward the ditch, wriggling himself out of the hole and rolling full-length on the ground toward the ditch. He expected every minute to hear the crack of a rifle and feel the tearing impact of its bullet in his flesh. He gained the ditch and lay listening. The diversion in the huts had reached a new crescendo of noise.

He picked up his kitbag and ran blindly toward the pine forest on the other side of the road from where the three of them started on the long trip home.

DAY KEENE (1904-   )

. . . who was born in Chicago became an actor at 16. He spent the next ten years of his life playing "every whistle stop east of the Mississippi River."

At 26, Day Keene turned to writing. His short stories were published in such diversified magazines as Dime Detective, Good Housekeeping, Liberty, *and* Esquire. *After a stint doing soap operas, he retired to Florida where he concentrated on writing novels—some 60 to date. These have been published in 12 languages.*

Mr. Keene, who now lives in North Hollywood, California, is still turning out two or three novels a year, the latest being L. A. 46 *and* Miami 59.

Only Mysto the Great could

REMEMBER THE NIGHT

and find the swag

MAX ENGLES was a tough, smart cop. He knew all the angles. It said so in the newspaper. That is, he had been a smart cop until too little salary, too many fifths of free whiskey, and a red-haired woman from St. Louis with a yen for a diamond ring had turned him into a portrait of the north end of a horse headed south.

There was even an old picture of the guy, a big black-haired Irishman, weighing perhaps two hundred and twenty pounds. I showed the picture to the barman.

"Who's this guy Engles?" I asked. "And what's all the fuss about? It says here he was bounced off the force eight years ago. Why the big write-up now?"

He was a slimy little punk with a good opinion of

himself. He'd also been out at the carnival lot the night before and it pleased him to rub it in. "Not so smart, are you, Carney? That's one time you slipped up." He quoted the banner in front of my pitch: *"The Great Mysto. Knows all. Sees all. Tells all. Reveals both the past and the future."*

There were four other men in the bar, a working stiff and three well-dressed lads who looked like hoods. The barman let them in on the joke. "Them Carneys is all alike. Fakers. This old gray-haired Joe works for the Greater Worthan Shows, claims he can read the past and the future. So he has to ask about Engles!" He grinned at me. "You're so good, Mysto, why don't you grab a shovel and go dig up the two hundred grand?"

I pretended to look him over carefully. "Engles is just a name to me. But take you, for example. I could tell you a lot about yourself."

He hooted. "I betcha."

I slapped a ten on the bar. "A bet." I nodded at the well-dressed lads. "And I'll let these gentlemen judge."

He covered my money, grinning. "Okay, Carney. Where was I born?"

I put the tips of my fingers to my forehead, closed my eyes, and concentrated. "In Aleppo, Syria. You came to this country with your family when you were four and moved here to Morgantown when you were fifteen. You live at One-three-two-six Forty-third Street South. You've been tending bar here for three months. You get sixty-two fifty a week and what you can steal. Last week you made a play for a big blonde named Mabel in the Hotel Gordon Grill but tried to make time too fast and got your face slapped. You bank at the Second National. Your passbook number is six-four-three-two-eight-one-five. And you have four hundred and twenty dollars and fifty-six cents on deposit."

I shook myself out of the trance and looked at him. His cheeks were beaded with sweat as he gaped at me.

"That enough?" I asked. "Or do you want more? I skipped over some things like that hot-car rap, for example, your dishonorable discharge from the Army, and that black-haired little married waitress who—"

"Shut up," he managed finally, red in the face. "For God's sake, shut up!"

I looked at one of the well-dressed lads. "My money?"

He said, "So it would seem." He asked the barman, "That was straight stuff he was giving you?"

The barman still wasn't convinced. "He couldn't know all that. I never told no one I was Syrian, or where I was born, or how old I was when I come to this country."

It was my time to crow. "I'm the Great Mysto. Remember? The past, the present and the future are an open book to me."

The well-dressed lad asked the barman if he had his bankbook. He laid it on the bar. Both the number on the book and the amount of deposit checked with the figures I'd given. Shaking his head, the lad said, "I'd say the ten is yours." He was no longer unimpressed. "But tell me—how do you do it?"

I said truthfully, "I don't do it with mirrors."

Putting the ten in my wallet, I picked the newspaper off the bar and limped out of the place.

There was a nip in the air, but that far south it doesn't really get cold. I was comfortable wearing a suit coat. From what I had seen of it, Morgantown looked like it would be a good stand. A town of around one hundred thousand population, its streets were comfortably filled with shoppers. Stores and the bars and the movie houses and the March of Dimes layout on the corner of Broad Street and First Avenue were doing a fair business.

I laid a dime on the board and asked the guy at the mike for the name of a good place to eat. He thanked me for the drive and recommended Daly's. I read more about Max Engles as I ate. It was quite a story. Engles, it seemed, had been a lieutenant on the local vice squad, vice in Morgantown being a general term embracing everything from gambling and the illicit handling of liquor to its more accepted definition. He had also been the man who carried the little black bag into which the bad boys and girls dropped their weekly donations if they wanted to stay in business. The funny part of it was, according to the story in the paper, even Engles' worst enemies admitted he had been an honest cop, living on his small salary, never taking a dime for himself —until he had fallen in love with and married a red-haired night-club entertainer from St. Louis.

The reporter who wrote the story used that theme throughout. *"St. Louis woman wid her diamon' rings.*

*... pulls dat man roun' by her apron strings."**
.. pulls dat man roun' by her apron strings."*

A child, a girl whom they had named Ailine, had been born to them. And that had been the beginning-of-the-end department. Suddenly imbued with the preposterous idea that the wife and child of a lieutenant of detectives ought to live on a scale commensurate with the molls of the racketeers from whom he was collecting tribute, and the over-fed wives and mistresses of the crooked police department heads and city officials to whom he was turning it over, Engles had blown his top and started to dip into the little black bag.

It couldn't last. It didn't. The more he stole the more he had to steal to chink up the cracks in the cages to keep the tigers in the City Hall from realizing the amount of red meat he was snatching from under their noses.

The end came when Engles' kid got sick. The doctors diagnosed it as this and that. By the time it developed it was polio and Ailine was desperately in need of an iron lung—and there wasn't one in Morgantown—Lieutenant Engles, for all he had stolen, was too broke to have one flown in. He had appealed to his superiors, but since they were suspicious of him now, the crowd in the City Hall had turned him down.

Now came the crux of the story. Desperate, he had got roaring drunk and gone on an unscheduled collection. The town had never known such a shakedown. It was, put it in the pot—or else.

The newspaper estimated that in his twelve-hour

tour of the gambling joints, gin mills, bookies, and call-houses with something to hide, Lieutenant Engles had collected in the neighborhood of two hundred thousand dollars.

The waiter brought me a fresh cup of coffee. "I see now," I told him, "what the town is talking about."

He looked over my shoulder at the paper. "Oh, you mean that Engles affair. Yeah. The paper prints that every year. Kind of a moral lesson like, I guess. You know—it don't pay to steal. And how your dime may make an iron lung available to some kid that needs one."

I read on and saw why the barman had said if I was as good as I claimed to be I'd go buy myself a shovel.

The money hadn't done Ailine any good. She died sometime during Engles' tour. And somehow he'd heard of it. When they caught up with him he was crying, fighting drunk, but he hadn't the money and refused to say what he'd done with it.

The paper said he'd been called on the carpet, severely reprimanded, then dismissed from the force. Knowing a little about how crooked police departments operate, I knew he'd also had the hell beat out of him, trying to make him tell where the money was.

There was more, but I didn't bother to read it. I folded the paper and drank my coffee. "What happened to Engles?"

The waiter shook his head. "No one seems to know. Him and his wife left town and ain't been heard from since. Although I did meet a marine in a bar one night who claimed to have seen a guy who looked like Engles with a Seabee outfit in the South Pacific. But you know how it was. Before he could make sure, his outfit was moved on."

"And the money was never found?" I said.

"Not a cent."

I suggested maybe Engles and his wife had taken the money with them, and the waiter laughed in my face.

"That just shows you don't know this town, mister. I bet the wolves that run it stripped both of them to the hide and went over 'em with a vacuum cleaner and a Geiger counter before they even let 'em get past the first traffic light."

I asked if he meant to tell me the same gang Engles had collected for were still in office.

He was apologetic. "You know how the voters are, mister. When something bad breaks in the paper they get all excited and hold mass meetings and reform rallies. But it never lasts. And that was eight years ago. As long as the millage isn't raised, Uncle John is put on home relief, and someone quashes parking tickets, they don't really care who's in City Hall."

When I got back to the lot, Lou was drinking coffee in the trailer, her freshly bleached hair in little fat curls all over her head, her face smeared with muscle cream. She asked how the town looked.

I tossed her the paper. "Wdie open, baby. A lot of chatter about two hundred grand lying around loose, finders-keepers."

I looked at her for a long time. "Lou," I said, "how

would you like to throw this pitch out the window? Maybe head down Florida way and do nothing the rest of our lives but lie on the sand and listen to the waves?"

She wasn't too enthused. "That would take money, wouldn't it?"

Ignoring the front page of the paper and the story about Max Engles, she found the crossword puzzle and started penciling it in.

It was going to rain, and hard. I could tell it by my leg. The afternoon had been a strain. I started to say something nasty, to touch off some reaction in her, then decided it was best to forget it.

Without looking up from the puzzle, she said. "The cards are in the pocket of your dress coat."

I skimmed through them while I dressed because I couldn't take them with me. Except for names and dates and places they all contained almost identical data. Given a taking-off point, I could almost do without them.

Tying my white tie, I studied my face in the mirror. The Great Mysto was getting old. It was small wonder Lou no longer enthused over my coming or going. It was small wonder the punk in the bar had called me an old gray-haired Joe. I was. My hair was a dirty white, and thinning. My wisp of a waxed mustache was ludicrous. I had lines in my face deep enough to lay a lead pencil in. My shoulders were thin and stooped. My one hundred and thirty-five pounds was mostly sallow skin and bones and nerves.

I poured myself a stiff drink, then stooped to kiss

Lou goodbye. She turned away. "Be careful of your coat. My face is greasy."

I asked if she wasn't going to wish me luck.

"You," she said, "are the mind reader."

I let it go at that and walked over to the tent. I'd been right about Morgantown. It was a good stand. Business was even better than it had been the night before. None of the special pigeons showed up to be plucked, but the run-of-the-midway were satisfied to be told, at two bucks the telling, the usual things they want to hear.

I'd just finished a special five-dollar reading, when the well-dressed lad I had met in the bar came in.

"Okay. Let's go, Mysto," he told me. "There's a guy in town who wants to talk to you."

I said I was highly flattered, but with four clients waiting I hadn't time at the moment to give an off-of-the-midway reading.

He showed me the butt of the gun in the holster under his arm. "That's up to you, fellow. My orders are to bring you in. I intend to. But I'd rather not get rough about it." He laid a C-note on the table. "Look. My name is Jimmy Conley. I'm only a working stiff— I take orders. Come see the guy and the C-note is yours for the favor. If you two can do business you'll get nine more like the one on the table. If it's no dice I'll drive you back and you keep the C-note for your trouble."

"And if I don't?"

"I'll have to get rough."

I picked the bill from the table and my hat from the

couch. "In that case, let's go, my friend. Believe me, Mr.
Conley, your argument is irresistible."

Conley only looked like a hood. He wasn't. He was,
it developed, a captain of detectives, and from what I
gleaned during the short ride he was currently toting
the little black bag that Max Engles had once carried.

Going up in the elevator at Central Bureau, I asked,
"You're sure this isn't a pinch? I bought my reader."
And I showed him my license to tell fortunes in Mor-
gantown.

"No. It isn't a pinch," he assured me.

Pushing open a door on the fourth floor he led me
through an anteroom into a large office. A fat man sitting back of a desk looked me over and didn't seem to
think much of what he saw.

"So you're the Great Mysto. You're the man who
knows all, sees all, tells all. All right. Tell me who I
am."

I said, "You're Chief of Police Sam Shalley."

"And how did you know that?"

"Your name is on the door."

A tall, dark man was sitting with one haunch on the
desk. He said, "A clown. A wise Carney. Okay, tell
me who I am."

"That," I admitted, "comes harder." I concentrated
for a few seconds. "But the name McElroy comes to
me. And the name is followed by the fourth and first
letter of the alphabet."

Shalley was impressed.

The D.A. was amused. "Sure he knows who we are.

All Carneys take particular care to identify the fuzz. Most of them have a dame out in front of their pitch. She blows into town three or four days before the show comes in." He explained it as though to a child. "It's her job to pick up pigeons. She learns all she can about them. Then when Mysto here hits town the stupes are so amazed by the facts he knows about them they not only are willing to pay anything he asks to learn their future, they give him a thousand dollars' worth of free advertising. . . . Isn't that the way you work it, fellow?"

I said, "You're telling the story."

Police Chief Shalley seemed disappointed.

I turned to Conley. "Okay, chum. It looks like I get a free ride back to the lot. That was the agreement, wasn't it? It looks like the boys have changed their minds about wanting me to help locate the money Engles stashed away."

"How did you know that?" Shalley gasped.

He looked at Conley. Conley shook his head. "I didn't tell him a thing."

"How *did* you know?' 'the D.A. asked.

I snapped, "I'm the Great Mysto. Remember? I reveal both the post and the future. And it would seem you *do* have a confidential problem." I put on my hat. "Well, nice to have met you gentlemen. I'll probably see you in jail sometime."

I started for the door and Shalley told Conley to stop me. His fat face was as red as a spanked baby's fanny. "Just one minute, Mysto. You heard the D.A. *How did you know what I had in mind?* Talk or I'll slap you in the lock-up and throw away the key."

He could do it.

"The story about Engles is all over the front page of the evening paper," I told him. "It says he must have collected close to two hundred thousand dollars, but there's nothing in the story to indicate the money was ever recovered. Ergo, it's still to be found."

Shalley asked McElroy what ergo meant.

"What's your right name, Mysto?" McElroy asked.

Captain Conley answered before I could. "He gave it as Beemis on his reader, Joe Beemis."

"Frisk him, Captain," McElroy ordered. "Check the name against his driver's license and any other identification in his wallet."

I handed Conley my wallet. He went through it and reported that the name on the miniature copy of my Seabee discharge and all my other papers check with the name on my reader.

Shalley laughed until his corporation bobbled. "Wha did you do in the Seabees, Mysto?"

"It wasn't reading minds."

"How about a record?" McElroy asked. "Have you a record, Mysto?" McElroy was the smartest cookie of the three and he had a pot cooking on his own back burner. It was in his eyes.

I told the truth. "A few misdemeanor raps in towns where the fuzz refused to stay paid. Nothing on the big book."

He rolled an unlighted cigar between his lips for a long time before he spoke again. Then, looking at Con-

ley, he said, "That will be all for you, Captain. I think
the chief and I can handle this from now on."

Conley shrugged and left the office.

When he had gone, McElroy returned his attention
to me. "How about it, Mysto? Think you can help us
locate that money?"

I played it for what it was worth. "I haven't the least
idea. But even if I knew I could, I wouldn't do it for a
grand. It wouldn't be worth my trouble. That's only
one half of one per cent of two hundred thousand dollars."

He waived my objection aside. "We won't quibble.
Locate the money and you can name your fee."

Shalley shook his head. "But you said he was a fake."

The D.A. smiled indulgently. "I have been wrong.
And you heard what Conley said. Mysto told the at-
tendant in the Glass Bar things the barman swore he
had never told anyone."

"That was different," I pointed out. "The barman
was there. I could read his mind. Where is this Engles
now? How do I get to him?"

"That," McElroy said, "is your problem. We aren't
interested in Engles. What we want is the money. And
unless—which I doubt very much—he slipped back into
town sometime during the past eight years and recovered it, it's still buried here somewhere. He was covered
with mud when we picked him up. Mud. Concentrate
on mud."

I said, "Okay. But mud is mud. Give me some other,
more personal, point of departure. How about this red-

haired woman mentioned in the paper?"

"We don't know where she is, either."

I thought a moment. Then I asked Shalley if he had anything that Engles had ever handled.

He said, "Hell, no," then corrected himself. "Say! I might at that." He took a box from the bottom drawer of his desk, sorted through the junk in it, and tossed a silver shield on the blotter. "There. That was Max's buzzer. Will that help you any?"

I played it cagey. "It might."

Both of them watching me, I limped over to the couch and sat on the edge of the circle of light formed by the lamp on Shalley's desk. Then, cupping the shield in my left hand, I closed my eyes and pressed the tips of the fingers of my right hand to my forehead.

It's funny the things you can see when you close your eyes and think hard. The shield came alive in my hand. I could see Max Engles distinctly—big, burly, loud-mouthed, ignorant, black-haired and barrel-chested, as he was in the newspaper picture on the day he had first got his shield.

Then the picture of Engles began to change. There were lines in his face. He was older, not so cocky. He'd been given the little black bag and he didn't quite know what to do about it. What he was doing was wrong. He knew it. But an order was an order and he couldn't lose his new commission.

Mud. Mud. Concentrate on mud.

The pictures began to run in slightly faster sequence, like those thrown by an old-fashioned motion picture projector that was getting out of hand.

I could hear music, laughter. A singing woman jerked across the screen. A young woman, red-haired, smiling, offering her lips to Engles. Then I saw his fingers dip into the little black bag and the shield in my hand turned hot.

The sequence of scenes ran still faster. The screen was streaked with rain. A child cried fitfully, stopped. A woman screamed. Then still big, still burly, roaring drunk, Engles took up all of the screen staggering swiftly through the rain and night, carrying the little black bag.

The tempo increased to the heat and madness of fever. The child was no longer crying but Engles was. Now he was kneeling in the mud in prayer. Now he was back on his feet shaking his fists at the sky. Now, hidden by a high board fence and the night, a sly, drunken smile on his lips while tears washed the rain from his cheeks, he was digging, faster, faster, faster . . .

The speeding film broke. The screen flooded with light. I tried to stand up and my knees gave way, pitching me onto my face. Both Shalley and McElroy let me lay.

When I could, I got to my feet.

"Quite a performance," the D.A. said.

Shalley licked his thick lips. "Well?"

I asked, "Is there a ball park in town? Surrounded by a high board fence covered with advertising?"

McElroy slapped his thigh. "The old ball park—of course! The boys picked up Max two blocks from there.

But there's no ball park now—"

"They've got the memorial there," Shalley said. "The names of all the guys who went into service. On the big white billboard."

"The league franchise wasn't picked up, so they tore down the ball park and made a public park out of the area," McElroy said. "They put up this memorial board and installed those big lights." He snapped his fingers. "As far as I know the lights that illuminate the memorial have never been turned off since. That's why Max couldn't go back and dig up the money!"

He turned to me. "Did it come to you just where Max buried the dough? Or do we dig up the park?"

I shook my head. "Not if you remember where home plate was. I can work from there."

He smiled. "Not from here?"

"I'd have to be there. The next point of departure."

The D.A. considered a moment. Then he picked up the phone on the Chief's desk, called the City Power Plant, and asked to speak to the engineer in charge. His call completed, he told Shalley to get some of the city police maps—both old and new—out of the plat file. He studied them carefully, then said, "Okay. Let's go dig."

It was raining lightly when we left Central Bureau. There weren't too many people on the street, but a flat-bed covered truck was backed up to the March of Dimes layout and a sister team was going to town with "Riders in the Sky" while the guy handling the sidewalk mike beat the drum.

We rode in McElroy's car. Shalley had been enthused in the office. Most of it waned by the time we neared the park. He rode in the back seat muttering to himself. Once I heard him say, "What the hell? How could a guy just sit there holding a buzzer in his hand and figure out where two hundred grand is buried?"

You could see the lights of the memorial eight blocks away. The D.A. drove around the park, estimating the number of people. Most of the town was at the carnival, I guess. Finally we parked and sat there in the car.

Shalley asked, "Now what do we do?"

The D.A. said, "Wait. Until the lights are turned off we're in the same predicament poor Max Engles has been in for eight years. If Rolph Welch, or any of the boys who put up that money, knew we were on the trail . . ."

For some reason he began to sweat. He wiped his face with his pocket handkerchief. Then taking a pint bottle from the glove compartment of the car he took a stiff drink and passed the bottle to Shalley.

While he was drinking the lights went out. Not only the park lights but the street and house lights as well.

"We have," McElroy announced, "about half an hour."

He got a shovel from the back of the car and led the way across the street and into the park. We could hear young voices wondering what had happened, and other young voices that were happy about the whole thing. We went past the tall billboard, and I had a vagrant thought about the names on the small, white plaques.

"Okay, Mysto," McElroy grunted. I heard the rustle of paper as he studied the maps beneath the thin beam of the flashlight he'd brought from the car. He stood on a piece of lawn about fifteen yards from the memorial and said, "This is it. Home plate was here."

There wasn't time or light enough for any acting. I oriented myself, then took six steps toward where the netting had been. "Dig here."

He handed me the shovel. "No, you dig. I wouldn't deprive you of the privilege." As I dug he kept up a steady stream of low-pitched conversation. "You must have been wounded in the Seabees, eh, Mysto?"

I said I'd lost part of a leg.

He sympathized, "And a lot of weight, too, I'll bet you. I managed to stay out of it myself. But I know how it must have been. It aged a lot of men before their time. Yes. There's nothing like war to turn a man's hair white and carve new lines in his face. You know, they say some men came back so changed even their old friends were hard put to recognize them."

I stopped digging.

He dug his gun into my spine. "Keep right on digging. You're doing fine."

It was all over Police Chief Shalley's head. He wanted to know what McElroy was getting at.

The D.A. told him, simply. "Money."

My shovel blade grated on metal. I scooped the loose dirt away and lifted out a five-gallon can. It felt like it was rusted in places but I couldn't feel any holes that went through. I started to pry off the top and McElroy hit me a vicious swipe across the face with his gun.

"No. Let the chief do that, Mysto."

I lay where the blow had knocked me, spitting blood, and hating him. Then I heard a squeak of metal and Shalley babbled, "The guy isn't a fake. It's here. Max's bag is in the can."

McElroy shushed him, "Not so loud, you fat fool!"

But he was almost as excited as Shalley. Neither of them saw nor heard the deeper blob of moving night move across the lawn until the other man was almost on them.

"That's nice," the newcomer admired. "If I were you boys, I'd freeze in that position. On you, it looks good."

McElroy's voice was strained. He sounded as though his throat hurt him. "What are you doing here, Rolph?"

The other man told him. "Me? I'm following a tip. Some Carney who called himself The Great Mysto phoned me just before it got dark and said he had a psychic message that if I were to show up at the old ball park tonight and all the lights in the city went out, he wouldn't be at all surprised if I found two guys digging up Engles' little black bag. It kinda intrigued me. And what do you know, he was right."

It was too dark to see much but he must have held out his free hand. "All right, McElroy. Hand it over."

McElroy stalled. "Now, wait, Rolph. We've been played for chumps. We—"

"How?" the racketeer asked. "This guy Mysto gave me a good tip." He grew impatient. "Come on. You can unfreeze enough to hand over that bag. I put up a lot of that dough in the first place."

Shalley lost his head. "No," he bleated. "Don't give it to him! Half of that money is mine. Shoot the dirty crook, Mac! We can square it."

And that was it.

McElroy screamed, "Shut up, you fool!" Too late.

Turning on my left side so my body hid the flash I'd slipped out my belly gun and fired two shots into the mud.

They were followed by a third, a fourth, and then a fifth shot.

His fingers laced over his belly, Rolph squatted as though he was doing a knee bend. But once down on his haunches he stayed there until he toppled over on his side.

McElroy was a tall man. He swayed like a flag pole in a high wind. With a tremendous effort of will he lifted the gun that had killed Rolph and leveled it at me. Before he could pull the trigger, it sagged. A moment later it thudded to the mud and he followed it to lie across the knees of the man who had killed him.

I slipped my gun back in my belt, got to my feet, and picked up the bag.

Shalley snatched at it, bleating. "No, you don't. You're under arrest."

I asked, "For what? I didn't shoot anyone." I was suddenly sick of the whole affair. "Now let go of the bag, fat boy, or I *will* stick around. And I'll tell the Grand Jury about a kid named Jenny. Remember the one the wagon boys carried out after that night party in an apartment over on B Street?"

He deflated like a punctured tire.

"What do you know about that?"

"Are you surprised," I told him. "I'm the Great Mysto. Remember?"

He still didn't get the score but he let go of the bag. The shots had been heard and reported. Men were shouting now along the street. In the distance I could hear the first rain-muted wail of a prowl car.

I walked through the rain to LeMoyne, and down LeMoyne three blocks to the car that I'd parked there shortly after I'd baited my trap in the Glass Bar. A trench coat covered my muddy tails. Conley might do a lot of thinking but it wouldn't get the kid anywhere. I was clean. No one could prove a damn thing.

All I had to do was drive on back to the lot and pick up Lou and the trailer. The Great Mysto had made his last pitch. Yet instead of moving on I sat there looking at the bag. It was eight years older and covered with mould. But it hadn't changed. It still was only money. I closed my eyes for a moment. And once more it was funny the things a guy can see when he closes his eyes and thinks hard.

The rain had let up a little but there was no one on the Midway and all of the joints had shut down for the night. I walked on into the trailer. Lou had dressed, but she was still working a crossword puzzle.

She looked up. "Well?"

"I had it. I had it right in my hand."

"What do you mean you *had* it?"

"Just that. Florida is out. We move on with the show," I told her.

She noticed the dried blood on my face for the first time. "You mean you had it and you let that gang of thieves take it away from you?"

I took off the trench coat and hung it on a hook. My evening clothes were a mess. I'd have to have them cleaned, maybe even buy a new set of tails, before I could make a pitch. "No. No one took it away from me. McElroy is dead. So is Rolph. And I'm in the clear. I had the damn bag in the car with me but I had to pass First and Broad to get here." She'd been down town that afternoon. I hoped she'd understand a little. "And there was a young guy out there in the rain beating the drum for dimes while a couple of kids about as old as Ailine would have been, shilled for his pitch. And, well, like I say, it was raining. And business was bad. So—" I tried to go on, and couldn't. I reached for the bottle.

Lou took it from me. "No. Please."

I wondered why I'd thought her eyes were hard. They weren't. They were blue and soft and swimming with tears. Then I realized it had been years since I had seen her cry.

She said, "So you laid the little black bag on the line."

I nodded. "Yeah."

Her being as close as she was I could see the red roots of the hairs the bleach had missed. I was almost afraid to ask. "Okay, sweetheart?"

"Okay, sweetheart?" she asked me. Her eyes were shining through the tears now. "You ask *me* if that's okay? I think that's just swell, Max."

She kissed me, hard. And suddenly neither of us were old, and all the wasted years had dropped away and things were as they once had been and life wasn't over at all. It was just beginning for both of us.

Lou buried her face on my chest. "I'll bet the guy was surprised."

"I wouldn't know," I told her. "I didn't stick around."

JOHN RUSSELL (1885-1956)

. . . was the son of an Iowa publicist. He became the
New York Herald's *special war correspondent in
Latin America before he was 23. Not long afterwards, he directed U.S. government wartime propa-
ganda in the British Isles.*

*Russell has written more than 600 short stories, most
o fthem adventures located in exotic areas.*

Karaki, the Melanesian, paid

a strange fee indeed as

THE PRICE OF THE HEAD

THE POSSESSIONS of Christopher Alexander Pellett
were these: his name, which he was always careful to
retain intact; a suit of ducks, no longer intact, in which
he lived and slept; a continuous thirst for liquor, and
a set of red whiskers. Also he had a friend. Now no
man can gain friendship, even among the gentle islands
of Polynesia, except by virtue of some quality attach-
ing to him. Strength, humor, villainy: he must show
some trait by which the friend can catch and hold.
How, then, explain the loving devotion lavished upon
Christopher Alexander Pellett by Karaki, the company
boat boy? This was the mystery at Fufuti.

There was no harm in Pellett. He never quarrelled.
He never raised his fist. Apparently he had never

learned that a white man's foot, though it wabble ever
so, is given him wherewith to kick natives out of the
road. He never even cursed anyone except himself and
the Chinese half-caste who sold him brandy, which was
certainly allowable because the brandy was very bad.

On the other hand, there was no perceptible good
in him. He had long lost the will to toil, and lately even
the skill to beg. He did not smile, nor dance, nor ex-
hibit any of the amiable eccentricities that sometimes
recommend the drunken to a certain toleration. In any
other part of the world he must have passed without
a struggle. But some chance had drifted him to the
beaches where life is as easy as a song and his particular
fate had given him a friend. And so he persisted. That
was all. He persisted, a sodden lump of flesh preserved
in alcohol.

Karaki, his friend, was a heathen from Bougainville,
where some people are smoked and others eaten. Being
a black, a Melanesian, he was as much an alien in brown
Fufuti as any white. He was a serious, efficient little
man with deeply sunken eyes, a great mop of kinky
hair, and a complete absence of expression. His tastes
were simple. He wore a red cotton kerchief belted
around his waist and a brass curtain ring suspended
from his nose.

Some powerful chief in his home island had sold
Karaki into the service of the trading company for
three years, annexing his salary of tobacco and beads
in advance. When the time should be accomplished,
Karaki would be shipped back to Bougainville, a mat-

ter of some eight hundred miles, where he would land no richer than before except in experience. This was the custom. Karaki may have had plans of his own.

It is seldom that one of the black races of the Pacific shows any of the virtues for which subject populations are admired. Fidelity and humility can be exacted from other colors between tan and chocolate. But the black remains the inscrutable savage. His secret heart is his own. Hence the astonishment of Fufuti, which knew the ways of black recruits, when Karaki took the worthless beachcomber to his bosom.

"Hy, you, Johnny," called Moy Jack, the Chinese half-caste. "Better you come catch this fella mahster b'long you. He fella plenty too much drunk galow."

Karaki left the shade of the copra shed where he had been waiting an hour or more and came forward to receive the sagging bulk that was thrust out of doors. He took it scientifically by wrist and armpit and swung toward the beach. Moy Jack stood on his threshold watching with cynic interest.

"Hy, you," he said; "what name you make so much bobeley 'long that fella mahster? S'pose you bling me all them fella pearl; me pay you one dam fella good trade—my word!"

It annoyed Moy Jack that he had to provide the white man with a daily drunk in exchange for the little seed pearls with which Pellett was always flush. He knew where those pearls came from. Karaki did forbidden diving in the lagoon to get them. Moy Jack made a good thing of the traffic, but he could have made a much better thing by trading directly with Karaki for a few sticks of tobacco.

"What name you give that fella mahster all them fella pearl?" demanded Moy Jack offensively. "He plenty too much no good, galow. Close up he die altogether."

Karaki did not reply. He looked at Moy Jack once, and the half-caste trailed off into mutterings. For an instant there showed a strange light in Karaki's dull eyes, like the flat, green flicker of a turning shark glimpsed ten fathoms down.

Karaki bore his charge down the beach to the little thatched shelter of pandanus leaves that was all his home. Tenderly he eased Pellett to a mat, pillowed his head, bathed him with cool water, brushed the filth from his hair and whiskers. Pellett's whiskers were true whiskers, the kind that sprout like the barbels of a catfish, and they were a glorious coppery, sun-gilt red. Karaki combed them out with a sandalwood comb. Later he sat by with a fan and kept the flies from the bloated face of the drunkard.

It was a little past midday when something brought him scurrying into the open. For weeks he had been studying every weather sign. He knew that the change was due when the southeast trade begins to harden through this flawed belt of calms and cross-winds. And now, as he watched, the sharp shadows began to blur along the sands and a film crept over the face of the sun.

All Fufuti was asleep. The house boys snored in the

back veranda. Under his netting the agent dreamed happily of big copra shipments and bonuses. Moy Jack dozed among his bottles. Nobody would have been mad enough to stir abroad in the noon hour of repose: nobody but Karaki, the untamed black, who cared nothing for custom nor yet for dreams. The light pad of his steps was lost in the surf drone on the barrier reefs. He flitted to and fro like a wraith. And while Fufuti slept he applied himself to a job for which he had never been hired.

Karaki had long ago ascertained two vital facts: where the key to the trade-room was kept and where the rifles and ammunition were hidden. He opened the trade-room and selected three bolts of turkey red cloth, a few knives, two cases of tobacco, and a fine small axe. There was much else he might have taken as well. But Karaki was a man of simple tastes, and efficient.

With the axe he next forced the rifle chest and removed therefrom one Winchester and a big box of cartridges. With the axe again he broke into the boat-sheds. Finally with the axe he smashed the bottoms out of the whaleboat and the two cutters so they would be of no use to anyone for many days to come. It was really a very handy little axe, a true tomahawk, ground to a shaving edge. Karaki took a workman's pleasure in its keen, deep strokes. It was almost his chief prize.

On the beach lay a big proa, a stout outrigger canoe of the kind Karaki's own people used at Bougainville, so high of prow and stern as to be nearly crescent-shaped. The northwest monsoon of last season had washed it ashore at Fufuti and Karaki had repaired it, by the agent's own order. This proa he now launched in the lagoon, and aboard it he stored his loot.

Of supplies he had to make a hasty selection. He took a bag of rice and another of sweet potatoes. He took as many coconuts as he could carry in a net in three trips. He took a cask of water and a box of biscuit. And here happened an odd thing.

In his search for the biscuit he came upon the agent's private store of liquor, a dozen bottles of rare Irish whisky. He glanced at them and passed them by. He knew what the stuff was, and he was a savage, a black man. But he passed it by. When Moy Jack heard of that later he remembered what he had seen in Karaki's eyes and ventured the surprising prediction that Karaki would never be taken alive.

When all was ready Karaki went back to his thatch and aroused Christopher Alexander Pellett.

"Hy, mahster, you come 'long me."

Mr. Pellett sat up and looked at him. That is to say, he looked. Whether he saw anything or not belongs among the obscurer questions of psychopathy.

"Too late," said Mr. Pellett profoundly. "This shop is closed. Copy boy! Give all those damned loafers good night. I'm—I'm goin'—bed!"

Whereupon he fell flat on his back.

"Wake up, mahster," insisted Karaki, shaking him. "You too much strong fella sleep. Hy-ah, mahster! Rum! You like'm rum? You catch'm rum any amount —my word! Plenty rum, mahster!"

But even this magic call, which never failed to rouse Pellett from his couch in the mornings, fell now on deaf ears. Pellett had had his skinful, and the fitness of things decreed that he should soak the clock around.

Karaki knelt beside him, pried him up until he could get a shoulder under his middle, and lifted him like a loose bag of meal. Pellett weighed one hundred and fifty pounds; Karaki not much more than a hundred. Yet in some deft coolie fashion of his own the little black man packed his burden, with the feet dragging behind, clear down to the beach. Moreover, he managed to get it aboard the proa. Pellett was half drowned and the proa half swamped. But Karaki managed.

No man saw their departure. Fufuti still dreamed on. Long before the agent awoke to wrath and ruin their queer crescent craft had slipped from the lagoon and faded away on the wings of the trade.

The first day Karaki had all he could do to keep the proa running straight before the wind. Big smoky seas came piling up out of the southeast and would have piled aboard if he had given them the least chance. He was only a heathen who did not know a compass from a degree of latitude. But his forefathers used to people these waters on cockleshell voyages that made the venture of Columbus look like a ride in a ferryboat. Karaki bailed with a tin pan and sailed with a mat and steered with a paddle: but he proceeded.

Along about sunrise Mr. Pellett stirred in the bilge and raised a pea-green face. He took one bewildered glance overside at the seething waste and collapsed with a groan. After a decent interval he tried again, but this was an illusion that would not pass, and he twisted around to Karaki sitting crouched and all aglisten with spray in the stern.

"Rum!" he demanded.

Karaki shook his head, and a haunted look crept into Pellett's eyes.

"Take—take away all that stuff," he begged pathetically, pointing at the ocean.

Thereafter for two days he was very, very sick, and he learned how a small boat in any kind of a sea can move forty-seven different ways within one and the same minute. This was no trifling bit of knowledge, as those who have acquired it can tell. It was nearly fatal to Pellett.

On the third day he awoke with a mouth and a stomach of fumed leather and a great weakness, but otherwise in command of his few faculties. The gale had fallen and Karaki was quietly preparing fresh coconuts. Pellett quaffed two before he thought to miss the brandy with which his breakfast draught was always laced. But when he remembered the milk choked in his throat.

"Me like'm rum."

"No got'm rum."

Pellett looked forward and aft, to windward and to lee. There was a great deal of horizon in sight, but nothing else. For the first time he was aware of a strangeness in events.

"What name you come so far?" he asked.

"We catch'm one big fella wind," explained Karaki.

Pellett was in no condition to question his statement nor to observe from the careful stocking of the proa that they had not been blown to sea on a casual fishing trip. Pellett had other things to think of. Some of the things were pink and others purple and others were striped like the rainbow in most surprising designs, and all were highly novel and interesting. They came thronging up out of the vasty deep to entertain Christopher Alexander Pellett. Which they did.

You cannot cut off alcohol from a man who has been continuously pickled for two years without results more or less picturesque. These were days when the proa went shouting across the empty southern seas to madrigal and choric song. Tied hand and foot and lashed under a thwart, Pellett raved in the numbers of his innocent youth. It would have been singular hearing had there been any to hear, but there was only Karaki, who did not care for the lesser Cavalier poets and on whom whole pages of "Atalanta in Calydon" were quite wasted. Now and then he threw a dipperful of sea water over the white man, or spread a mat to keep the sun from him, or fed him with coconut milk by force. Karaki was a poor audience, but an excellent nurse. Also, he combed Pellett's whiskers twice every day.

They ran into calms. But the trade picked them up again more gently, so that Karaki ventured to make westing, and they fled under skies as bright as polished brass.

"My heart is within me
As an ash in the fire;
Whosoever hath seen me
Without lute, without lyre,
Shall sing of me grievous things,
even things that were ill
to desire—"

Thus chanted Christopher Alexander Pellett, whose
face began to show a little more like flesh and a little
less like rotten kelp.

Whenever a fair chance offered, Karaki landed on
the lee of some one of the tiny islets with which the
Santa Cruz region is peppered, and would make shift
to cook rice and potatoes in the tin dipper. This was
risky, for one day the islet proved to be inhabited. Two
white men in a cutter came out to stop them. Karaki
could not hide his resemblance to a runaway nigger,
and he did not try to. But when the cutter approached
within fifty yards he suddenly announced himself as a
runaway nigger with a gun. He left the cutter sinking
and one of the men dead.

"There's a bullet hole alongside me here," said Pellett from under the thwart. "You'd better plug it."

Karaki plugged it and released his passenger, who
sat up and began stretching himself with a certain naive
curiosity of his own body.

"So you're real," observed Pellett, staring hard at
Karaki. "By George, you *are,* and that's comfort."

He was right. Karaki was very real.

"What side you take'm this fella canoe?"

"Balbi," said Karaki, using the native word for Bougainville.

Pellett whistled. An eight-hundred-mile evasion in an open boat was a considerable undertaking. It enlisted his respect. Moreover, he had just had emphatic proof of the efficiency of this little black man.

"Balbi all some home b'long you?"

"Yes."

"All right, commodore," said Pellett. "Lead on. I don't know why you shipped me for supercargo, but I'll see you through."

Strangely—or perhaps not so strangely—the whole Fufuti interval of his history had been fading from his brain while the poison was ebbing from his tissues. The Christopher Alexander Pellett that emerged was one from earlier years: pretty much of a wreck, it was true, and a feckless, indolent, paltry creature at best, but ordinarily human and rather more than ordinarily intelligent.

He was very feeble at first, but Karaki's diet of coconuts and sweet potatoes did wonders for him, and the time came when he could rejoice in the good salt taste of the spray on his lips and forget for hours together the crazy craving for stimulant. They made a strange crew, this pair—simple savage and convalescent drunkard—but there was never any question as to which was in command. That was well seen in the third week when their food began to fail and Pellett noticed that Karaki ate nothing for a whole day.

"See here, this won't do," he cried. "You've given

me the last coconut and kept none for yourself."

"Me no like'm eat," said Karaki shortly.

Christopher Alexander Pellett pondered many matters in long, idle hours while the rush of foam under the proa and the creak and fling of her outriggers were the only sounds between sea and sky. Sometimes his brow was knotted with pain. It is not always pleasant to be wrenched back into level contact with one's memories. Thoughts are no sweeter company for having long been drowned. He had met the horrors of delirium. He had now to face the livelier devils of his past. He had fled them before.

But here was no escape of any kind. So he turned and grappled with them and laid them one by one.

When they had been at sea twenty-nine days they had nothing left of their provisions but a little water. Karaki doled it out by moistening a shred of coconut husk and giving Pellett the shred to suck. In spite of Pellett's petulant protest, he would take none himself. Again the heathen nursed the derelict, this time through the last stages of thirst, scraping the staves of the cask and feeding him the ultimate drop of moisture on the point of a knife.

On the thirty-sixth day from Fufuti they sighted Choiseul, a great green wall that built up slowly across the west.

Once fairly under its headlands, Karaki might have indulged a certain triumph. He had taken as his target the whole length of the Solomons, some six hundred miles. But to have fetched the broadside of them anywhere in such a craft as the proa through storm and current, without instrument or chart, was distinctly a feat of navigation. Karaki, however, did no celebrating. Instead, he stared long and anxiously over his shoulder into the east.

The wind had been fitful since morning. By noon it was dead calm on a restless, oily sea. A barometer would have told evil tales, but Karaki must have guessed them anyway, for he staggered forward and unstepped the little mast. Then he bound all his cargo securely under the thwarts and put all his remaining strength into the paddle, heading for a small outpost island where a line of white showed beach. They had been very lucky thus far, but they were still two miles offshore when the first rush of the hurricane caught them.

Karaki himself was reduced to a rattle of bones in a dried skin, and Pellett could scarce lift a hand. But Karaki fought for Pellett among the waves that leaped up like sheets of fire on the reef. Why or how they got through neither could have said. Perhaps because it was written that after drink, illness, madness, and starvation the white man should be saved by the black man again and a last time from ravening waters. When they came ashore on the islet they were both nearly flayed, but they were alive, and Karaki still gripped Pellett's shirt.

For a week they stayed while Pellett fattened on unlimited coconut and Karaki tinkered the proa. It had landed in a water-logged tangle, but Karaki's treasures were safe. He got his bearings from a passing native fisherman, and then he knew that *all* his treasures were safe. His home island lay across Bougainville Strait, the stretch of water just beyond.

"Balbi over there?" asked Pellett.

"Yes," said Karaki.

"And a mighty good thing too," cried Pellett heartily. "This is the limit of British authority, old boy. Big fella mahster b'long Beretani stop'm here, no can go that side."

Karaki was quite aware of it. If he feared one thing in the world, he feared the Fiji High Court and its Resident Commissioner for the Southern Solomons, who did sure justice upon all who transgressed in its jurisdiction. Once beyond the strait he might still be liable for the stolen goods and the broken contract. But never—this was the point—never could he be punished for anything he might choose to do over there in Bougainville.

So Karaki was content.

And so was Christopher Alexander Pellett. His body had been wrung and swept and scoured, and he had downed his devils. Sweet air and sunshine were on his lips and in his heart. His bones were sweet in him. As his vigor returned he swam the lagoon or helped Karaki at the proa. He would spend hours hugging the warm sand or rejoicing in the delicate tracery of some tiny sea-shell, singing softly to himself, while the ground-swell hushed along the beach, savoring life as he never had done.

"Oh, this is good—good!" he said.

Karaki puzzled him. Not that he vexed himself, for a smiling wonder at everything, almost childlike, filled him these days. But he thought of this taciturn savage, how he had capped thankless service with rarest sacrifice. And now that he could consider soberly, the why of it eluded him. Why? Affection? Friendship? It must be so, and he warmed toward the silent little man with the sunken eyes and the expressionless face from which he could never raise a wink.

"Hy, you, Karaki, what name you no laugh all same me? What? You too much fright 'long that fella stuff you steal? Forget it, you old black scamp. If they ever trouble you, I'll square them somehow. By George, I'll say I stole it myself!"

Karaki only grunted and sat down to clean his Winchester with a bit of rag and some drops of oil he had crushed from a dried coconut.

"No, that don't reach him either," murmured Pellett, baffled. "I'd like to know what's going on under that topknot of yours, old chap. You're like Kipling's cat, that walks by himself. God knows I'm not ungrateful. I wish I could show you—"

He sprang up.

"Karaki! He one big fella friend 'long you: savee? You one big fella friend 'long me: savee? We two dam' big fella friend, my word! . . . What?"

"Yes," said Karaki. No other response. He looked at Pellett and he looked away toward Bougainville. "Yes," he said, "my word," and went on cleaning his gun—the black islander, inscrutable, incomprehensible, an enigma always, and to the end.

The end came two days later at Bougainville.

Under a gorgeous dawn they came into a bay that opened before their prow as with jeweled arms of welcome. The land lay lapped in bright garments like a sleeper half awakened, all flushed and smiling, sensuous, intimate, thrilling with life, breathing warm scents—

These were some of the foolish phrases Pellett babbled to himself as he leaped ashore and ran up on a rocky point to see and to feel and to draw all the charm of the place to himself.

Meanwhile Karaki, that simple and efficient little man, was proceeding methodically about his own affairs. He landed his bolts of cloth, his tobacco, his knives, and the other loot. He landed his box of cartridges and his rifle and his fine tomahawk. The goods were somewhat damaged by sea water, but the weapons had been carefully cleaned and polished.

Pellett was declaiming poetry aloud to the alluring solitude when he was aware of a gentle footfall and turned, surprised, to find Karaki standing just behind him with the rifle at his hip and the axe in his hand.

"Well," said Pellett cheerfully, "what d'you want, old chappie?"

"Me like," said Karaki, while there gleamed in his eyes the strange light that Moy Jack had glimpsed there, like the flicker of a turning shark; "me like'm too much one fella head b'long you!"

"What? Head! Whose—my head?"

"Yes," said Karaki simply.

That was the way of it. That was all the mystery. The savage had fallen enamored of the head of the beachcomber, and Christopher Alexander Pellett had been betrayed by his fatal red whiskers. In Karaki's country a white man's head, well smoked, is a thing to be desired above wealth, above lands and chief-ship's fame, and the love of women. In all Karaki's country was no head like the head of Pellett. Therefore Karaki had served to win it with the patience and single faith of a Jacob. For this he had schemed and waited, committed theft and murder, expended sweat and cunning, starved and denied himself, nursed, watched, tended, fed, and saved his man that he might bring the head alive and on the hoof—so to speak—to the spot where he could remove it at leisure and enjoy the fruits of his labor in safety.

Pellett saw all this at a flash, understood it so far as any white could understand it: the whole elemental and stupendous simplicity of it. And standing there in his new strength and sanity under the fair promise of the morning, he gave a laugh that pealed across the waters and started the sea birds from their cliffs, the deep-throated laugh of a man who fathoms and accepts the last great jest.

For finally, by corrected list, the possessions of Christopher Alexander Pellett were these: his name still intact; the ruins of some rusty ducks; his precious red whiskers—and a soul which had been neatly recovered, renewed, refurbished, reanimated, and restored to him by his good friend Karaki.

> *"Thou shouldst die as he dies,*
> *For whom none sheddeth tears;*
> *Filling thine eyes*
> *And fulfilling thine ears*
> *With the brilliance . . . the bloom*
> *and the beauty . . ."*

Thus chanted Christopher Alexander Pellett over the waters of the bay, and then whirled, throwing wide his arms:

"Shoot, damn you! It's cheap at the price!"

THE FOURTH MAN

had a gimmick that kept them alive.

What was it?

THE RAFT might have been taken for a swath of cut sedge or a drifting tangle of roots as it slid out of the shadowy river mouth at dawn and dipped into the first ground swell. But while the sky brightened and the breeze came fresh offshore it picked away among shoals and swampy islets with purpose and direction, and when at last the sun leaped up and cleared his bright eye of the morning mists it had passed the wide entrance to the bay and stood to open sea.

It was a curious craft for such a venture, of a type that survives here and there in the obscure corners of the world. The coracle maker would have scorned it. The first navigating pithecanthrope built nearly as well with his log and bush. A mat of pandanus leaves served

139

for its sail and a paddle of niaouli wood for its helm. But it had a single point of real seaworthiness. Its twin floats, paired as a catamaran, were woven of reed bundles and bamboo sticks upon triple rows of bladders. It was light as a bladder itself, elastic, fit to ride any weather. One other quality this raft possessed which recommended it beyond all comfort and safety to its present crew. It was very nearly invisible. They had only to unstep its mast and lie flat in the cup of its soggy platform and they could not be spied half a mile away.

Four men occupied the raft. Three of them were white. Their bodies had been scored with brambles and blackened with dried blood, and on wrist and ankle they bore the black and wrinkled stain of the gyves. The hair upon them was long and matted. They wore only the rags of blue canvas uniforms. But they were whites, members of the superior race—members of a highly superior race according to those philosophers who rate criminal aberration as a form of genius.

The fourth was a man who had built the raft and was now sailing it. There was nothing superior about him. His skin was a layer of soot. His prognathous jaw carried out the angle of a low forehead. No line of beauty redeemed his lean limbs and knobby joints. Nature had set upon him her plainest stamp of inferiority, and his only attempts to relieve it were the twist of bark about his middle and the prong of pig ivory through the cartilage of his nose. Altogether a very ordinary specimen of one of the lowest branches of the human family—the Canaques of New Caledonia.

The three whites sat together well forward, and so they had sat in silence for hours. But at sunrise, as if some spell had been raised by the clang of that great copper gong in the east, they stirred and breathed deep of the salt air and looked at one another with hope in their haggard faces, and then back toward the land which was now no more than a gray-green smudge behind them.

"Friends," said the eldest, whose temples were bound with a scrap of crimson scarf, "Friends—the thing is done."

With a gesture like conjuring he produced from the breast of his tattered blouse three cigarettes, fresh and round, and offered them.

"Nippers!" cried the one at his right. "True nippers —name of a little good man! And here? Doctor, I always said you were a marvel. See if they be not new from the box!"

Dr. Dubosc smiled. Those who had known him in very different circumstances about the boulevards, the lobbies, the clubs, would have known him again and in spite of all disfigurement by that smile. And here, at the bottom of the earth, it had set him still apart in the prisons, the cobalt mines, the chain gangs of a community not much given to mirth. Many a crowded lecture hall in Montpellier had seen him touch some intellectual firework with just a twinkle behind his bristly gray brows, with just such a thin curl of the lip.

"By way of celebration," he explained. "Consider.

There are seventy-five evasions from Noumea every six months, of which not more than one succeeds. I had the figures myself from Dr. Pierre at the infirmary. He is not much of a physician, but a very honest fellow. Could anybody win on that percentage without dissipating? I ask you."

"Therefore you prepared for this?"

"It is now three weeks since I bribed the night guard to get these same nippers."

The other regarded him with admiration. Sentiment came readily upon this beardless face, tender and languid, but overdrawn, with eyes too large and soft and mouth too long. It was one of those faces familiar enough to the police which might serve as model for an angel were it not associated with some revolting piece of deviltry. Fenayrou himself had been condemned "to perpetuity" as an incorrigible.

"Is not our doctor a wonder?" he inquired as he handed a cigarette along to the third white man. "He thinks of everything. You should be ashamed to grumble. See—we are free, after all. Free!"

The third was a gross, pock-marked man with hairless lids, known sometimes as Niniche, Troit Huit, Le Tordeur, but chiefly among copains as Perroquet—a name derived perhaps from his beaked nose, or from some perception of his jailbird character. He was a garroter by profession, accustomed to rely upon his fists only for the exchange of amenities. Dubosc might indulge a fancy and Fenayrou seek to carry it as a pose, but The Parrot remained a gentleman of strictly serious turn. There is perhaps a tribute to the practical spirit of penal administration in the fact that while Dubosc was the most dangerous of these three and Fenayrou the most depraved, Perroquet was the one with the official reputation, whose escape would be signaled first among the "Wanted." He accepted the cigarette because he was glad to get it, but he said nothing until Dubosc passed a tin box of matches and tne first gulp of picadura filled his lungs. . . .

"Wait till you ve got your two feet on a pavé, my boy. That will be the time to talk of freedom. What? Suppose there came a storm."

"It is not the season of storms," observed Dubosc

But The Parrot's word had given them a check. Such spirits as these, to whom the land had been a horror, would be slow to feel the terror of the sea. Back there they had left the festering limbo of a convict colony, oblivion. Out here they had reached the rosy threshold of the big round world again. They were men raised from the dead, charged with all the furious appetites of lost years, with the savor of life strong and sweet on their lips. And yet they paused and looked about in quickened perception, with the clutch at the throat that takes landsmen on big waters. The spaces were so wide and empty. The voices in their ears were so wide and murmurous. There was a threat in each wave that came from the depths, a sinister vibration. None of them knew the sea. None knew its ways, what tricks it might play, what traps it might spread—more deadly than those of the jungle.

The raft was running now before a brisk chop with alternate spring and wallow, while the froth bubbled in over the prow and ran down among them as they sat.

"Where is that cursed ship that was to meet us here?" demanded Fenayrou.

"It will meet us right enough." Dubosc spoke carelessly, though behind the blown wisp of his cigarette he had been searching the outer horizon with keen glance. "This is the day, as agreed. We will be picked up off the mouth of the river."

"You say," growled Perroquet. "But where is any river now? Or any mouth? Sacred name! this wind will blow us to China if we keep on."

"We dare not lie in any closer. There is a government launch at Torrien. Also the traders go armed hereabouts, ready for chaps like us. And don't imagine that the native trackers have given us up. They are likely to be following still in their proas."

"So far!"

Fenayrou laughed, for The Parrot's dread of their savage enemies had a morbid tinge.

"Take care, Perroquet. They will eat you yet."

"Is it true?" demanded the other, appealing to Dubosc. "I have heard it is even permitted these devils to keep all runaways they can capture—Name of God!—to fatten on."

"An idle tale," smiled Dubosc. "They prefer the reward. But one hears of convicts being badly mauled. There was a forester who made a break from Baie du

Sud and came back lacking an arm. Certainly these people have not lost the habit of cannibalism."

"Piecemeal," chuckled Fenayrou. "They will only sample you, Perroquet. Let them make a stew of your brains. You would miss nothing."

But The Parrot swore.

"Name of a name—what brutes!" he said, and by a gesture recalled the presence of that fourth man who was of their party and yet so completely separated from them that they had almost forgotten him.

The Canaque was steering the raft. He sat crouched at the stern, his body glistening like varnished ebony with spray. He held the steering paddle, immobile as an image, his eyes fixed upon the course ahead.

There was no trace whatever of expression on his face, no hint of what he thought or felt or whether he thought or felt anything. He seemed not even aware of their regard, and each one of them experienced somehow that twinge of uneasiness with which the white always confronts his brother of color—this enigma brown or yellow or black he is fated never wholly to understand or to fathom. . . .

"It occurs to me," said Fenayrou in a pause, "that our friend here who looks like a shiny boot is able to steer us God knows where. Perhaps to claim the reward."

"Reassure yourself," answered Dubosc. "He steers by my order. Besides, it is a simple creature—an infant, truly, incapable of any but the most primitive reasoning."

"Is he incapable of treachery?"

"Of any that would deceive us. Also, he is bound by his duty. I made my bargain with his chief, up the river, and this one is sent to deliver us on board our ship. It is the only interest he has in us."

"And he will do it. Such is the nature of the native."

"I am glad you feel so," returned Fenayrou, adjusting himself indolently among the drier reeds and nursing the last of his cigarette. "For my part I wouldn't trust a figurehead like that for two sous. Mazette! What a monkey face!"

"Brute!" repeated Perroquet, and this man, sprung from some vile river-front slum of Argenteuil, whose home had been the dock pilings, the grog shop, and the jail, even this man viewed the black Canaque from an immeasurable distance with the look of hatred and contempt. . . .

Under the heat of the day the two younger convicts lapsed presently into dozing. But Dubosc did not doze. His tormented soul peered out behind its mask as he stood to sweep the sky line again under shaded hand. His theory had been so precise, the fact was so different. He had counted absolutely on meeting the ship—some small schooner, one of those flitting, half-piratical traders of the copra islands that can be hired like cabs in a dark street for any questionable enterprise. Now there was no ship, and here was no crossroads where one might sit and wait. Such a craft as the catamaran could not be made to lie to.

The doctor foresaw ugly complications for which

he had prepared and whereof he must bear the whole burden. The escape had been his own conception, directed by him from the start. He had picked his companions deliberately from the whole forced labor squad, Perroquet for his great strength, Fenayrou as a ready echo. He had made it plain since their first dash from the mine, during their skirmish with the military guards, their subsequent wanderings in the brush with bloodhounds and trackers on the trail—through every crisis—that he alone should be the leader.

For the others, they had understood well enough which of their number was the chief beneficiary. Those mysterious friends on the outside that were reaching half round the world to further their release had never heard of such individuals as Fenayrou and The Parrot. Dubosc was the man who had pulled the wires: that brilliant physician whose conviction for murder had followed so sensationally, so scandalously, upon his sweep of academic and social honors. There would be clacking tongues in many a Parisian salon, and white faces in some, when news should come of his escape. Ah, yes, for example, they knew the highflyer of the band, and they submitted—so long as he led them to victory. They submitted, while reserving a depth of jealousy, the inevitable remnant of caste still persisting in this democracy of stripes and shame.

By the middle of the afternoon the doctor had taken certain necessary measures.

"Ho," said Fenayrou sleepily. "Behold our colors at the masthead. What is that for, comrade?"

"To help them sight us when the ship comes."

"What wisdom!" cried Fenayrou. "Always he thinks of everything, our doctor; everything—"

He stopped with the phrase on his lips and his hand outstretched toward the center of the platform. Here, in a damp depression among the reeds, had lain the wicker-covered bottle of green glass in which they carried their water. It was gone.

"Where is that flask?" he demanded. "The sun has grilled me like a bone."

"You will have to grill some more," said Dubosc grimly. "This crew is put on rations."

Fenayrou stared at him wide-eyed, and from the shadow of a folded mat The Parrot thrust his purpled face. "What do you sing me there? Where is that water?"

"I have it," said Dubosc.

They saw, in fact, that he held the flask between his knees, along with their single packet of food in its wrapping of cocoanut husk.

"I want a drink," challenged Perroquet.

"Reflect a little. We must guard our supplies like reasonable men. One does not know how long we may be floating here. . . ."

Fell a silence among them, heavy and strained, in which they heard only the squeaking of the frail basket-work as their raft labored in the wash. Slow as was their progress, they were being pushed steadily outward and onward, and the last cliffs of New Caledonia were no longer even a smudge in the west, but only a hazy line. And still they had seen no moving thing upon the great round breast of the sea that gleamed in its corselet of brass plates under a brazen sun.

"So that is the way you talk now?" began The Parrot, half choking. "You do not know how long? But you were sure enough when we started."

"I am still sure," returned Dubosc. "The ship will come. Only she cannot stay for us in one spot. She will be cruising to and fro until she intercepts us. We must wait."

"Ah, good! We must wait. And in the meantime, what? Fry here in the sacred heat with our tongues hanging out while you deal us drop by drop—*hein?*"

"Perhaps."

"But no!" The garroter clenched his hands. "Blood of God, there is no man big enough to feed me with a spoon!"

Fenayrou's chuckle came pat, as it had more than once, and Dubosc shrugged.

"You laugh?" cried Perroquet, turning in fury. "But how about this Lascar of a captain that lets us put to sea unprovided? What? He thinks of everything, does he? He thinks of everything! . . . Sacred farceur—let me hear you laugh again!"

Somehow Fenayrou was not so minded.

"And now he bids us be reasonable," concluded The Parrot. "Tell that to the devils in hell. You and your cigarettes, too. Bah—comedian!"

"It is true," muttered Fenayrou, frowning. "A bad piece of work for a captain of runaways."

But the doctor faced mutiny with his thin smile.

"All this alters nothing. Unless we would die very speedily, we must guard our water."

"By whose fault?"

"Mine," acknowledged the doctor. "I admit it. What then? We can't turn back. Here we are. Here we must stay. We can only do our best with what we have."

"I want a drink," repeated The Parrot, whose throat was afire since he had been denied.

"You can claim your share, of course. But take warning of one thing. After it is gone, do not think to sponge on us—on Fenayrou and me."

"He would be capable of it, the pig!" exclaimed Fenayrou, to whom this thrust had been directed. "I know him. See here, the doctor is right. Fair for one, fair for all."

"I want a drink."

Dubosc removed the wooden plug from the flask.

"Very well," he said quietly.

With the delicacy that lent something of legerdemain to all his gestures, he took out a small canvas wallet, the crude equivalent of the professional black bag, from which he drew a thimble. Meticulously he poured a brimming measure, and Fenayrou gave a shout at the grumbler's fallen jaw as he accepted that tiny cup between his big fingers. Dubosc served Fenayrou and himself with the same amount before he re-corked the bottle.

"In this way we should have enough to last us three days—maybe more—with equal shares among the three of us."

Such was his summing of the demonstration, and it passed without comment, as a matter of course in the premises, that he should count as he did—ignoring that other who sat alone at the stern of the raft, the black Canaque, the fourth man.

Perroquet had been outmaneuvered, but he listened sullenly while for the hundredth time Dubosc recited his easy and definite plan for their rescue, as arranged with his secret correspondents.

"That sounds very well," observed The Parrot at last. "But what if these jokers only mock themselves of you. What if they have counted it good riddance to let you rot here? And us? Sacred name, that would be a famous jest! To let us wait for a ship and they have no ship!"

"Perhaps the doctor knows better than we how sure a source he counts upon," suggested Fenayrou slyly.

"That is so," said Dubosc with great good humor. "My faith, it would not be well for them to fail me. Figure to yourselves that there is a safety vault in Paris full of papers to be opened at my death. Certain friends of mine could hardly afford to have some little confessions published that would be found there. . . . Such a tale as this, for instance—"

And to amuse them he told an indecent anecdote of high life, true or fictitious, it mattered nothing, so he could make Fenayrou's eyes glitter and The Parrot growl in wonder. Therein lay his means of ascendancy over such men, the knack of eloquence and vision.

Harried, worn, oppressed by fears that he could sense so much more sharply than they, he must expend himself now in vulgar marvels to distract these ruder minds. He succeeded so far that when the wind fell at sunset they were almost cheerful, ready to believe that the morning would bring relief. They dined on dry biscuit and another thimbleful of water apiece and took watch by amiable agreement. And through that long clear night of stars, whenever the one of the three who lay awake between his comrades chanced to look aft, he could see the vague blot of another figure—the naked Canaque, who slumbered there apart.

It was an evil dawning. Fenayrou, on the morning trick, was aroused by a foot as hard as a hoof, and started up at Perroquet's wrathful face, with the doctor's graver glance behind.

"Idler! Good-for-nothing! Will you wake at least before I smash your ribs? Name of God, here is a way to stand watch!"

"Keep off!" cried Fenayrou wildly. "Keep off! Don't touch me!"

"Eh, and why not, fool? Do you know that the ship could have missed us? A ship could have passed us a dozen times while you slept!"

"*Bourrique!*"

"*Vache!*"

They spat the insults of the prison while Perroquet knotted his great fists over the other, who crouched away catlike, his mobile mouth twisted to a snarl. Dubosc stood aside in watchful calculation until against

the angry red sunrise in which they floated there flashed
the naked red gleam of steel. Then he stepped between.

"Enough. Fenayrou, put up that knife."

"The dog kicked me."

"You were at fault," said Dubosc sternly. "Perroquet!"

"Are we all to die that he may sleep?" stormed The
Parrot.

"The harm is done. Listen now, both of you. Things
are bad enough already. We may need all our energies.
Look about."

They looked and saw the far, round horizon and the
empty desert of the sea and their own long shadows that
slipped slowly before them over its smooth, slow heav-
ing, and nothing else. The land had sunk away from
them in the night—some one of the chance currents that
sweep among the islands had drawn them none could
say where or how far. The trap had been sprung.

"Good God, how lonely it is!" breathed Fenayrou in
a hush.

No more was said. They dropped their quarrel. Silently they shared their rations as before, made shift to
eat something with their few drops of water, and sat
down to pit themselves one against another in the vital
struggle that each could feel was coming—a sort of tacit
test of endurance.

A calm had fallen as it does between trades in this
flawed belt, an absolute calm. The air hung weighted.
The sea showed no faintest crinkle, only the madden-
ing, unresting heave and fall in polished undulations

on which the lances of the sun broke and drove in under their eyelids as white, hot splinters; a savage sun that kindled upon them with the power of a burning glass, that sucked the moisture from poor human bits of jelly and sent them crawling to the shelter of their mats and brought them out again, gasping, to shrivel anew. The water, the world of water, seemed sleek and thick as oil. They came to loathe it and the rotting smell of it, and when the doctor made them dip themselves overside they found little comfort. It was warm and sluggish, slimed. But a curious thing resulted. . . .

While they clung along the edge of the raft they all faced inboard, and there sat the black Canaque. He did not join them. He did not glance at them. He sat hunkered on his heels in the way of the native, with arms hugging his knees. He stayed in his place at the stern, motionless under that shattering sun, gazing out into vacancy. Whenever they raised their eyes, they saw him. He was the only thing to see.

"Here is one who appears to enjoy himself quite well," remarked Dubosc.

"I was thinking so myself," said Fenayrou.

"The animal!" rumbled Perroquet.

They observed him, and for the first time with direct interest, with thought of him as a fellow being—with the beginning of envy.

"He does not seem to suffer."

"What is going on in his brain? What does he dream of there? One would say he despises us."

"The beast!"

"Perhaps he is waiting for us to die," suggested Fenayrou with a harsh chuckle. "Perhaps he is waiting for the reward. He would not starve on the way home at least. And he could deliver us—piecemeal."

They studied him.

"How does he do it, doctor? Has he no feeling?"

"I have been wondering," said Dubosc. "It may be that his fibers are tougher—his nerves."

"Yet we have had water and he none."

"But look at his skin, fresh and moist."

"And his belly, fat as a football!"

The Parrot hauled himself aboard.

"Don't tell me this black beast knows thirst!" he cried with a strange excitement. "Is there any way he could steal our supplies?"

"Certainly not."

"Then, name of a dog, what if he has supplies of his own hidden about?"

The same monstrous notion struck them all, and the others swarmed to help. They knocked the black aside. They searched the platform where he sat, burrowing among the rushes, seeking some hidden cache, another bottle or a gourd. They found nothing.

"We were mistaken," said Dubosc.

But Perroquet had a different expression for disappointment. He turned on the Canaque and caught him by the kinky mop of hair and proceeded to give him what is known as gruel in the cobalt mines. This was a little specialty of The Parrot's. He paused only when he himself was breathless and exhausted and threw the limp, unresisting body from him.

"There, lump of dirt! That will teach you. Maybe you're not so chipper now, my boy—*hein?* Not quite so satisfied with your luck. Pig! That will make you feel. . . ."

It was a ludicrous, a wanton, a witless thing. But the others said nothing. The learned Dubosc made no protest. Fenayrou had none of his usual jests at the garroter's stupidity. They looked on as at the satisfaction of a common grudge. The white trampled the black with or without cause, and that was natural. And the black crept away into his place with his hurts and his wrongs and made no sign and struck no blow. And that was natural too.

The sun declined into a blazing furnace whereof the gates stood wide, and they prayed to hasten it and cursed because it hung so long enchanted. But when it was gone their blistered bodies still held the heat like things incandescent. The night closed down over them like a purple bowl, glazed and impermeable. They would have divided the watches again, though none of them thought of sleep, but Fenayrou made a discovery.

"Idiots!" he rasped. "Why should we look and look? A whole navy of ships cannot help us now. If we are becalmed, why so are they!"

The Parrot was singularly put out.

"Is this true?" he asked Dubosc.

"Yes, we must hope for a breeze first."

"Then, name of God, why didn't you tell us so?

Why did you keep on playing out the farce?"

He pondered it for a time. "See here," he said. "You
are wise, eh? You are very wise. You know things we
do not and you keep them to yourself." He leaned forward to peer into the doctor's face. "Very good. But
if you think you are going to use that cursed smartness
to get the best of us in any way—see here, my zig, I
pull your gullet out like the string of an orange. . . .
Like that. What?"

Fenayrou gave a nervous giggle and Dubosc shrugged, but it was perhaps about this time that he began
to regret his intervention in the knife play.

For there was no breeze and there was no ship.

By the third morning each had sunk within himself,
away from the rest. The doctor was lost in a profound
depression, Perroquet in dark suspicion, and Fenayrou
in bodily suffering, which he supported ill. Only two
effective ties still bound their confederacy. One was the
flask which Dubosc had slung at his side by a strip of
wickerwork. Every move he made with it, every drop
he poured, was followed with burning eyes. And he
knew and he had no advantage of them in knowing
that the will to live was working its relentless formula
aboard that raft. Under his careful saving there still
remained nearly half of their original store.

The other bond, as it had come to be by strange
mutation, was the presence of the black Canaque.

There was no forgetting the fourth man now, no
overlooking him. He loomed upon their conscious-
ness, more formidable, more mysterious, more exas-

perating with every hour. Their own powers were ebbing. The naked savage had yet to give the slightest sign of complaint or weakness.

During the night he had stretched himself out on the platform as before, and after a time he had slept. Through the hours of darkness and silence while each of the whites wrestled with despair, this black man had slept as placidly as a child, with easy, regular breathing. Since then he had resumed his place aft. And so he remained, unchanged, a fixed fact and a growing wonder.

The brutal rage of Perroquet, in which he had vented his distorted hate of the native, had been followed by superstitious doubts.

"Doctor," he said at last, in awed huskiness, "is this a man or a fiend?"

"It is a man."

"A miracle," put in Fenayrou.

But the doctor lifted a finger in a way his pupils would have remembered.

"It is a man," he repeated, "and a very poor and wretched example of a man. You will find no lower type anywhere. Observe his cranial angle, the high ears, the heavy bones of his skull. He is scarcely above the ape. There are educated apes more intelligent."

"Ah? Then what?"

"He has a secret," said the doctor.

That was a word to transfix them.

"A secret! But we see him—every move he makes, every instant. What chance for a secret?"

The doctor rather forgot his audience, betrayed by chagrin and bitterness.

"How pitiful!" he mused. "Here are we three—children of the century, products of civilization—I fancy none would deny that, at least. And here is this man who belongs before the Stone Age. In a set trial of fitness, of wits, of resource, is he to win? Pitiful!"

"What kind of a secret?" demanded Perroquet, fuming.

"I cannot say," admitted Dubosc with a baffled gesture. "Possibly some method of breathing, some peculiar posture that operates to cheat the sensations of the body. Such things are known among primitive peoples—known and carefully guarded—like the properties of certain drugs, the uses of hypnotism and complex natural laws. Then, again, it may be psychologic—a mental attitude persistently held. Who knows? . . .

"To ask him? Useless. He will not tell. Why should he? We scorn him. We give him no share with us. We abuse him. He simply remains inscrutable—as he has always been and will always be. He never tells those innermost secrets. They are the means by which he has survived from the depth of time, by which he may yet survive when all our wisdom is dust."

"I know several very excellent ways of learning secrets," said Fenayrou as he passed his dry tongue over his lips. "Shall I begin?"

Dubosc came back with a start and looked at him.

"It would be useless. He could stand any torture you could invent. No, that is not the way."

"Listen to me," said Perroquet with sudden violence. "Me, I am wearied of the gab. You say he is a man. Very well. If he is a man, he must have blood in his veins. That would be, anyway, good to drink."

"No," returned Dubosc. "It would be hot. Also it would be salt. For food—perhaps. But we do not need food."

"Kill the animal then, and throw him over."

"We gain nothing."

"Well, sacred name, what do you want?"

"To beat him!" cried the doctor, curiously agitated. "To beat him at the game—that's what I want! For our own sakes, for our racial pride, we must, we must. To outlast him, to prove ourselves his masters. By better brain, by better organization and control. Watch him, watch him, friends—that we may ensnare him, that we may detect and defeat him in the end!"

But the doctor was miles beyond them.

"Watch?" growled The Parrot. "I believe you, old windbag. It is all one watch. I sleep no more and leave any man alone with that bottle."

To this the issue finally sharpened. Such craving among such men could not be stayed much longer by driblets. They watched. They watched the Canaque. They watched each other. And they watched the falling level in their flask—until the tension gave.

Another dawn upon the same dead calm, rising like a conflagration through the puddled air, cloudless, hopeless! Another day of blinding, slow-drawn agony to meet. And Dubosc announced that their allowance must be cut to half the thimbleful.

There remained perhaps a quarter of a liter—a miserable reprieve of bare life among the three of them, but one good swallow for a yearning throat.

At the sight of the bottle, at the tinkle of its limpid content, so cool and silvery green inside the glass, Fenayrou's nerves snapped.

"More!" he begged, with pleading hands. "I die. More!"

When the doctor refused him, he groveled among the reeds, then rose suddenly to his knees and tossed his arms abroad with a hoarse cry.

"A ship! A ship!"

The others spun about. They saw the thin, unbroken ring of this greater and more terrible prison to which they had exchanged; and that was all they saw, though they stared and stared. They turned back to Fenayrou and found him in the act of tilting the bottle. A cunning slash of his knife had loosed it from its sling at the doctor's side. . . . Even now he was sucking at the mouth, spilling the precious liquid—

With one sweep Perroquet caught up their paddle and flattened him, crushed him.

Springing across the prostrate man, Dubosc snatched the flask upright and put the width of the raft between himself and the big garroter who stood wide-legged, his bloodshot eyes alight, rumbling in his chest.

"There is no ship," said The Parrot. "There will be no ship. We are done. Because of you and your rotten promises that have brought us here—doctor, liar, ass!"

Dubosc stood firm.

"Come a step nearer and I break bottle and all over your head."

They stood regarding each other, and Perroquet's brows gathered in a slow effort of thought.

"Consider," urged Dubosc with his quaint touch of pedantry. "Why should you and I fight? We are rational men. We can see this trouble through and win yet. Such weather cannot last forever. Besides, here are only two of us to divide the water now."

"That is true," nodded The Parrot. "That is true, isn't it? Fenayrou kindly leaves us his share. An inheritance—what? A famous idea. I'll take mine now."

Dubosc probed him keenly.

"My share at once, if you please," insisted Perroquet, with heavy docility. "Afterwards we shall see. Afterwards."

The doctor smiled his grim and wan little smile.

"So be it."

Without relinquishing the flask, he brought out his canvas wallet once more—that wallet which replaced the professional black bag—and rolled out the thimble by some swift sleight of his flexible fingers while held Perroquet's glance with his own.

"I will measure it for you."

He poured the thimbleful and handed it over quickly, and when Perroquet had tossed it off he filled again and again.

"Four—five," he counted. "That is enough."

But The Parrot's big grip closed quietly around his

wrist at the last offering and pinioned him and held him helpless.

"No, it is not enough. Now I will take the rest. Ha, wise man! Have I fooled you at last?"

There was no chance to struggle and Dubosc did not try, only stayed smiling up at him, waiting.

Perroquet took the bottle.

"The best man wins," he remarked. "Eh, my zig? A bright notion of yours. The—best—"

His lips moved, but no sound issued. A look of the most intense surprise spread upon his round face. He stood swaying a moment, and collapsed like a huge hinged toy when the string is cut.

Dubosc stooped and caught the bottle again, looking down at his big adversary, who sprawled in a brief convulsion and lay still, a bluish scum oozing between his teeth. . . .

"Yes, the best man wins," repeated the doctor, and laughed as he in turn raised the flask for a draft.

"The best man wins!" echoed a voice in his ear.

Fenayrou, writhing up and striking like a wounded snake, drove the knife home between his shoulders.

The bottle fell and rolled to the middle of the platform, and there, while each strove vainly to reach it, it poured out its treasure in a tiny stream that trickled away and was lost.

It may have been minutes or hours later—for time has no count in emptiness—when next a sound proceeded from that frail slip of a raft, hung like a mote between sea and sky. It was a phrase of song, a wander-

ing strain in half tones and fluted accidentals, not un-
melodious. The Black Canaque was singing. He sang
without emotion or effort, quite casually and softly to
himself. So he might sing by his forest hut to ease some
hour of idleness. Clasping his knees and gazing out into
space, untroubled, unmoved, enigmatic to the end, he
sang—he sang.

And, after all, the ship came.

She came in a manner befitting the sauciest little
tops'l schooner between Nukahiva and the Pelews—as
her owner often averred and none but the envious denied—in a manner worthy too of that able Captain
Jean Guilbert, the merriest little scamp that ever
cleaned a pearl bank or snapped a cargo of labor from
a scowling coast. Before the first whiff out of the west
came the *Petite Suzanne,* curtsying and skipping along
with a flash of white frill by her forefoot, and brought
up startled and stood shaking her skirts and keeping
herself quite daintily to windward.

"And 'ere they are sure enough, by dam!" said the
polyglot Captain Jean in the language of commerce
and profanity. "Zose passengers for us, hey? They been
here all the time, not ten mile off—I bet you, Marteau.
Ain't it 'ell? What you zink, by gar?"

His second, a tall and excessively bony individual of
gloomy outlook, handed back the glasses.

"More bad luck. I never approved this job. And now
—see—we have had our voyage for nothing. What misfortune!"

"Marteau, if that good Saint Pierre gives you some

day a gold 'arp, still you would holler bad luck—bad job!" retorted Captain Jean. "Do I 'ire you to stand zere and cry about ze luck? Get a boat over, and quicker zan zat!"

M. Marteau aroused himself sufficiently to take command of the boat's crew that presently dropped away to investigate. . . .

"It is even as I thought," he called up from the quarter when he returned with his report. "I told you how it would be, Captain Jean."

"Hey?" Captain Jean cried, bouncing at the rail. "Have you got those passengers yet, *enfant de salaud?*"

"I have not," said Marteau in the tone of lugubrious triumph. There was nothing in the world that could have pleased him quite so much as this chance to prove Captain Jean the loser on a venture. "We are too late. Bad luck, bad luck—that calm. What misfortune! They are all dead!"

"Will you mind your business?" shouted the skipper.

"But still the gentlemen are dead—"

"What is zat to me? All ze better, they will cost nozing to feed."

"But how—"

"Hogsheads, my gar," said Captain Jean paternally. "Zose hogsheads in the afterhold. Fill them nicely with brine, and zere we are!" And after having drawn all possible satisfaction from the other's amazement, he sprang the nub of his joke with a grin. "Ze gentlemen's passage is all paid, Marteau. Before we left Sydney, Marteau. I contrac' to bring back three escape' convicts and so by 'ell I do—in pickle! And now if you'll kindly get zose passengers aboard like I said and bozzer less about ze goddam luck, I be much oblige'. Also, zere is no green on my eye, Marteau, and you can dam well smoke it!"

Marteau recovered himself with difficulty in time to recall another trifling detail. "There is a fourth man on board that raft, Captain Jean. He is a Canaque—still alive. What shall we do with him?"

"A Canaque?" snapped Captain Jean. "A Canaque! I had no word in my contrac' about any Canaque. . . . Leave him zere. . . . He is only o dam nigger. He'll do well enough where he is."

And Captain Jean was right, perfectly right, for while the *Petite Suzanne* was taking aboard her grisly cargo the wind freshened from the west, and just about the time she was shaping away for Australia the "dam nigger" spread his own sail of pandanus leaves and twirled his own helm of niaouli wood and headed the catamaran eastward, back toward New Caledonia.

Feeling somewhat dry after his exertions, he plucked at random from the platform a hollow reed with a sharp end and, stretching himself at full length in his accustomed place at the stern, he thrust the reed down into one of the bladders underneath and drank his fill of the sweet water. . . .

He had a dozen such storage bladders remaining, built into floats at intervals above the water line—quite enough to last him safely home again.

EDGAR ALLAN POE

... was orphaned at the age of two and, though never legally adopted, was given a home by a rich Scottish merchant, John Allan, whose name he combined with his own.

Shortly after he entered the University of Virginia, he got into trouble by gambling and drinking; from then on, Poe alternately distinguished himself with his writing and tormented himself with drink and his ever-present form of insanity.

Poe will always be celebrated as one of the truly great American writers and poets and, incidentally, as the founder of the modern detective story. George Bernard Shaw once called him "this finest of finest of artists."

"The Black Cat" is one of Poe's masterpieces. In fact, it is one of the masterpieces in English in the short story. Macabre, sensitive, and spine-chilling, this tale horrifies and fascinates.

A rope around the neck of

THE BLACK CAT

led to the hangman

FOR THE MOST wild yet most homely narrative which I am about to pen, I neither expect nor solicit belief. Mad indeed would I be to expect it, in a case where my very senses reject their own evidence. Yet, mad am I not—and very surely do I not dream. But tomorrow I die, and today I would unburden my soul.

My immediate purpose is to place before the world, plainly, succinctly, and without comment, a series of mere household events. In their consequences, these events have terrified—have tortured—have destroyed me. Yet I will not attempt to expound them. To me, they have presented little but horror—to many will they seem less terrible than *baroques*.

From my infancy I was noted for the docility and

humanity of my disposition. My tenderness of heart was even so conspicuous as to make me the jest of my companions. I was especially fond of animals, and was indulged by my parents with a great variety of pets. With these I spent most of my time, and never was so happy as when feeding and caressing them.

This peculiarity of character grew with my growth, and, in my manhood, I derived from it one of my principal sources of pleasure. To those who have cherished an affection for a faithful and sagacious dog, I need hardly take the trouble to explain the nature or the intensity of the gratification thus derivable. There is something in the unselfish and self-sacrificing love of a brute, which goes directly to the heart of him who has had frequent occasion to test the paltry friendship and gossamer fidelity of mere *man.*

I married early, and was happy to find in my wife a disposition congenial with my own. Observing my partiality for domestic pets, she lost no opportunity of procuring those of the most agreeable kind. We had birds, goldfish, a fine dog, rabbits, a small monkey, and a *cat.*

This latter was a remarkably large and beautiful animal, entirely black, and sagacious to an astonishing degree. In speaking of his intelligence, my wife, who at heart was not a little tinctured with superstition, made frequent allusion to the ancient popular notion, which regarded all black cats as witches in disguise.

Pluto—this was the cat's name—was my favorite pet and playmate. I alone fed him, and he attended me wherever I went about the house. It was even with difficulty that I prevented him from following me through the streets.

Our friendship lasted for several years, during which my general temperament and character—through the instrumentality of the Fiend Intemperance—had experienced a radical alteration for the worse.

Day by day, I grew more moody, more irritable, regardless of the feelings of others. I used intemperate language to my wife. At length, I even offered her personal violence.

My pets, of course, were made to feel the change in my disposition. I not only neglected, but ill-used them. For Pluto, however, I still retained sufficient regard to refrain from maltreating him, but I made no scruple of maltreating the rabbits, the monkey, or even the dog, when, by accident, or through affection, they got in my way. But my disease grew upon me—the disease of Alcohol!—and at length even Pluto, who was now becoming old, and consequently somewhat peevish—even Pluto began to experience the effects of my ill temper.

One night, returning home, much intoxicated, from one of my haunts about town, I fancied that the cat avoided my presence. I seized him; when, in his fright at my violence, he inflicted a slight wound upon my hand with his teeth.

The fury of a demon instantly possessed me. I knew myself no longer. My original soul seemed, at once, to take its flight from my body; and a more than fiendish malevolence, gin-nurtured, thrilled every fibre of my frame. I took from my waistcoat pocket a penknife, opened it, grasped the poor beast by the throat, and deliberately cut one of its eyes from the socket! I blush, I burn, I shudder, while I pen the damnable atrocity.

When reason returned with the morning—when I had slept off the fumes of the night's debauch—I experienced a sentiment half of horror, half of remorse, for the crime of which I had been guilty; but it was, at best, a feeble and equivocal feeling, and the soul remained untouched. I again plunged into excess, and soon drowned in wine all memory of the deed.

In the meantime the cat slowly recovered. The socket of the lost eye presented, it is true, a frightful appearance, but he no longer appeared to suffer any pain. He went about the house as usual, but, as might be expected, fled in extreme terror at my approach.

I had so much of my old heart left, as to be at first grieved by this evident dislike on the part of a creature which had once so loved me. But this feeling soon gave place to irritation. And then came, as if to my final and irrevocable overthrow, the spirit of *perverseness*. Of this spirit philosophy takes no account.

Who has not, a hundred times, found himself committing a vile or a stupid action, for no other reason than because he knows he should *not?* Have we not a perpetual inclination, in the teeth of our best judgment, to violate that which is *Law,* merely because we understand it to be such?

This spirit of perverseness, I say, came to my final overthrow. It was this unfathomable longing of the soul *to vex itself*—to offer violence to its own nature—to do wrong for the wrong's sake only—that urged me to continue and finally to consummate the injury I had inflicted upon the unoffending brute.

One morning, in cold blood, I slipped a noose about its neck and hung it to the limb of a tree—hung it with the tears streaming from my eyes, and with the bitterest remorse at my heart—hung it *because* I knew that it had loved me, and *because* I felt it had given me no reason of offense—hung it *because* I knew that in so doing I was committing a sin—a deadly sin that would so jeopardize my immortal soul as to place it—if such a thing were possible—even beyond the reach of the infinite mercy of the Most Merciful and Most Terrible God.

On the night of the day on which this most cruel deed was done, I was aroused from sleep by the cry of fire. The curtains of my bed were in flames. The whole house was blazing. It was with great difficulty that my wife, a servant, and myself, made our escape from the conflagration. The destruction was complete. My entire worldly wealth was swallowed up, and I resigned myself thenceforward to despair.

I am above the weakness of seeking to establish a sequence of cause and effect, between the disaster and the atrocity. But I am detailing a chain of facts—and wish not to leave even a possible link imperfect.

On the day succeeding the fire, I visited the ruins. The walls, with one exception, had fallen in. This exception was found in a compartment wall, not very thick, which stood about the middle of the house, and against which had rested the head of my bed. The plastering had here, in great measure, resisted the action of the fire—a fact which I attributed to its having been recently spread.

Around this wall a dense crown was collected, and many persons seemed to be examining a particular portion of it with minute and eager attention. The words "strange!" "singular!" and other similar expressions, excited my curiosity. I approached and saw, as if graven in bas-relief upon the white surface, the figure of a gigantic cat! The impression was given with an accuracy truly marvelous. There was a rope about the animal's neck.

When I first beheld this apparition—for I could scarcely regard it as less—my wonder and my terror were extreme. But at length reflection came to my aid. The cat, I remembered, had been hung in a garden adjacent to the house. Upon the alarm of fire, this garden had been immediately filled by the crowd—by some one of whom the animal must have been cut from the tree and thrown through an open window into my chamber. This had probably been done with the intention of arousing me from sleep. The falling of other walls had compressed the victim of my cruelty into the substance of the freshly-spread plaster; the lime of which, with the flames, and the *ammonia* from the carcass, had then accomplished the portraiture as I saw it.

Although I thus readily accounted to my reason, if

not altogether to my conscience, for the startling fact just detailed, it did not fail to make a deep impression upon my fancy.

For months I could not rid myself of the phantasm of the cat; and, during this period, there came back into my spirit a half-sentiment that seemed, but was not, remorse. I went so far as to regret the loss of the animal, and to look among the vile haunts which I now habitually frequented, for another pet of the same species, and of somewhat similar appearance, with which to supply its place.

One night as I sat half stupefied, in a den of more than infamy, my attention was suddenly drawn to some black object, reposing upon the head of one of the immense hogsheads of gin, or of rum, which constituted the chief furniture of the room.

I had been looking steadily at the top of this hogshead for some minutes, and what now caused me surprise was the fact that I had not sooner perceived the object thereupon. I approached it, and touched it with my hand. It was a black cat—a very large one—fully as large as Pluto, and closely resembling him in every respect but one. Pluto had not a white hair upon any portion of his body; but this cat had a large, although indefinite splotch of white, covering nearly the whole region of its breast.

Upon my touching him, he immediately arose, purred loudly, rubbed against my hand, and appeared delighted with my notice. This, then, was the very creature of which I was in search. I at once offered to buy it from the landlord; but this person made no claim to it—knew nothing of it—had never seen it before.

I continued my caresses, and when I prepared to go home, the animal evinced a disposition to accompany me. I permitted it to do so; occasionally stooping and patting it as I proceeded. When it reached the house it domesticated itself at once, and became immediately a great favorite with my wife.

For my own part, I soon found a dislike to it arising within me. This was just the reverse of what I had anticipated; but—I know not how or why it was—its evident fondness for me rather disgusted and annoyed me.

By slow degrees these feelings of disgust and annoyance rose into the bitterness of hatred. I avoided the creature; a certain sense of shame and the remembrance of my former deed of cruelty prevented me from physically abusing it. I did not, for some weeks, strike, or otherwise violently ill-use it; but gradually —very gradually—I came to look upon it with unutterable loathing, and to flee silently from its odious presence, as from the breath of a pestilence.

What added, no doubt, to my hatred of the beast, was the discovery, on the morning after I brought it home, that, like Pluto, it also had been deprived of one of its eyes. This circumstance, however, only endeared it to my wife, who, as I have already said, possessed, in a high degree, that humanity of feeling which had once been my distinguishing trait, and the source of many of my simplest and purest pleasures.

With my aversion to this cat, however, its partiality for me seemed to increase. It followed my footsteps with a pertinacity which it would be difficult to make the reader comprehend. Whenever I sat, it would crouch beneath my chair, or spring upon my knees, covering me with its loathsome caresses.

If I arose to walk, it would get between my feet and thus nearly throw me down; or fastening its long and sharp claws in my dress, clamber, in this manner, to my breast. At such times, although I longed to destroy it with a blow, I withheld from so doing, partly by a memory of my former crime, but chiefly—let me confess it at once—by absolute *dread* of the beast.

This dread was not exactly a dread of physical evil—and yet I should be at a loss how otherwise to define it. I am almost ashamed to own—yes, even in this felon's cell, I am almost ashamed to own—that the terror and horror with which the animal inspired me, had been heightened by one of the merest chimeras it would be possible to conceive.

My wife had called my attention, more than once, to the character of the mark of white hair, of which I have spoken, and which constituted the sole visible difference between the strange beast and the one I had destroyed. The reader will remember that this mark, although large, had been of indefinite shape. But, by slow degrees—nearly imperceptible, and which for a long time my reason struggled to reject as fanciful—it had, at length, assumed a rigorous distinctness of outline.

It was now the representation of an object that I shudder to name—and for this, above all, I loathed, and dreaded, and would have rid myself of the monster *had I dared*—it was now the image of a hideous—of a ghastly thing—of the GALLOWS!—oh, mournful and terrible engine of Horror and of Crime—of Agony and of Death!

And now was I indeed wretched beyond the wretchedness of mere Humanity. And *a brute beast*—whose fellow I had contemptuously destroyed—*a brute beast* to work out for *me*—for me, a man fashioned in the image of the High God—so much of insufferable woe!

Alas! neither by day nor by night knew I the blessing of rest any more! During the former the creature left me no moment alone, and in the latter I started hourly from dreams of unutterable fear to find the hot breath of *the thing* upon my face, and its vast weight—an incarnate nightmare that I had no power to shake off—incumbent eternally upon my *heart!*

Beneath the pressure of torments such as these the feeble remnant of the good within me succumbed. Evil thoughts became my sole intimates—the darkest and most evil of thoughts. The moodiness of my usual temper increased to hatred of all things and of all mankind; while from the sudden, frequent, and ungovernable outbursts of a fury to which I now blindly abandoned myself, my uncomplaining wife, alas, was the most usual and the most patient of sufferers.

One day she accompanied me, upon some household errand, into the cellar of the old building which our poverty compelled us to inhabit. The cat followed me down the steep stairs, and, nearly throwing me headlong, exasperated me to madness.

Lifting up an axe, and forgetting in my wrath the childish dread which had hitherto stayed my hand, I aimed a blow at the animal, which, of course, would have proved instantly fatal had it descended as I wished. But this blow was arrested by the hand of my wife. Goaded by the interference into a rage more than demoniacal, I withdrew my arm from her grasp and buried the axe in her brain. She fell dead upon the spot without a groan.

This hideous murder accomplished, I set myself forthwith, and with entire deliberation, to the task of concealing the body. I knew that I could not remove it from the house, either by day or by night, without the risk of being observed by the neighbors. Many projects entered my mind.

At one period I thought of cutting the corpse into minute fragments, and destroying them by fire. At another, I resolved to dig a grave for it in the floor of the cellar. Again, I deliberated about casting it into the well in the yard; about packing it in a box, as if merchandise, with the usual arrangements, and so getting a porter to take it from the house.

Finally I hit upon what I considered a far better expedient than any of these. I determined to wall it up in the cellar, as the monks of the Middle Ages are recorded to have walled up their victims.

For a purpose such as this, the cellar was well adapted. Its walls were loosely constructed, and had lately been plastered throughout with a rough plaster, which the dampness of the atmosphere had prevented from hardening. Moreover, in one of the walls was a projection, caused by a false chimney, or fireplace, that had been filled up and made to resemble the rest of the cellar. I had no doubt that I could readily displace the bricks at this point, insert the corpse, and wall the whole up as before, so that no eye could detect anything suspicious.

And in this calculation I was not deceived. By means of a crowbar I easily dislodged the bricks, and, having carefully deposited the body against the inner wall, I propped it in that position, while with little trouble I relaid the whole structure as it originally stood. Having procured mortar, sand, and hair, with every possible precaution, I prepared a plaster which could not be distinguished from the old, and with this I very carefully went over the new brickwork.

When I had finished, I felt satisfied that all was right. The wall did not present the slightest appearance of having ben disturbed. The rubbish on the floor was picked up with the minutest care. I looked around triumphantly, and said to myself: "Here at least, then, my labor has not been in vain."

My next step was to look for the beast which had been the cause of so much wretchedness; for I had, at length, firmly resolved to put it to death. Had I been able to meet with it at the moment, there could have been no doubt of its fate; but it appeared that the crafty animal had been alarmed at the violence of my previous anger, and forbore to present itself in my present mood.

It is impossible to describe or to imagine the deep, the blissful sense of relief which the absence of the detested creature occasioned in my bosom. It did not make its appearance during the night; and thus for one night, at least, since its introduction into the house, I soundly and tranquilly slept; aye, *slept* even with the burden of murder upon my soul.

The second and third day passed, and still my tormentor came not. Once again I breathed as a free man. The monster, in terror, had fled the premises for ever! I should behold it no more! My happiness was supreme!

The guilt of my dark deed disturbed me but little. Some few inquiries for my wife had been made, but these had been readily answered. Even a search had been instituted—but of course nothing was discovered. I looked upon my future felicity as secured.

Upon the fourth day of the assassination, a party of the police came into the house very unexpectedly, and proceeded again to make rigorous investigation of the premises. Secure, however, in the inscrutability of my place of concealment, I felt no embarrassment whatever.

The officers bade me accompany them in their search. They left no nook or corner unexplored. At length, for the third or fourth time, they descended into the cellar. I quivered not in a muscle. My heart beat calmly as that of one who slumbers in innocence.

I walked the cellar from end to end. I folded my arms upon my chest and roamed easily to and fro. The police were thoroughly satisfied and prepared to depart. The glee in my heart was too strong to be restrained. I burned to say if but one word, by way of triumph, and to render doubly sure their assurance of my guiltlessness.

"Gentlemen," I said at last, as the party ascended the steps, "I delight to have allayed your suspicions. I wish you all health and a little more courtesy. By the bye, gentlemen, this is a very well-constructed house,"—in the rabid desire to say something easily, I scarcely knew what I uttered at all—"I may say an *excellently* well-constructed house. These walls—are you going, gentlemen?—these walls are solidly put together," and through the mere frenzy of bravado, I rapped heavily with a cane which I held in my hand, upon the very portion of the brickwork behind which stood the corpse of the wife of my bosom.

But may God shield and deliver me from the fangs of the arch fiend! No sooner had the reverberation of my blows sunk into silence, than I was answered by a voice from within the tomb! By a cry, at first muffled and broken, like the sobbing of a child, and then quickly swelling into one long, loud, and continuous scream, utterly anomalous and inhuman—a howl—a wailing shriek, half of horror and half of triumph, such as might have arisen only out of hell, conjointly from the throats of the damned in their agony, and of the demons that exult in the damnation.

Of my own thoughts it is folly to speak. Swooning, I staggered to the opposite wall. For one instant the party on the stairs remained motionless, through extremity of terror and awe. In the next a dozen stout arms were toiling at the wall. It fell bodily.

The corpse, already greatly decayed and clotted with gore, stood erect before the eyes of the spectators. Upon its head, with red extended mouth and solitary eye of fire, sat the hideous beast whose craft had seduced me into murder, and whose informing voice had consigned me to the hangman.

I had walled the monster up within the tomb.

JAMES MALLAHAN CAIN (1892-   )

. . . was the son of a college president. After receiving his M.A. at the early age of 18, he worked as a reporter for the Baltimore American *and for the* Baltimore Sun.

During his reporting days he met H. L. Mencken, who encouraged him to become a fiction writer. Mencken published Cain's first short story in the American Mercury.

Cain went on to write full length magazine serials, one-act plays, and novels. With The Postman Always Rings Twice *he became a popular success. The film version of this and other novels brought him wealth and fame.*

All the facts of the tragedy

became clear when they found

THE BABY IN
THE ICE BOX

OF COURSE there was plenty pieces in the paper about what happened out at the place last summer, but they got it all mixed up, so I will now put down how it really was, and specially the beginning of it, so you will see it is not no lies in it.

Because when a guy and his wife begin to play leap-frog with a tiger, like you might say, and the papers put in about that part and not none of the stuff that started it off, and then one day say X marks the spot and next day say it wasn't really no murder but don't tell you what it was, why, I don't blame people if they figure there was something funny about it or maybe that somebody ought to be locked up in the booby hatch. But there wasn't no booby hatch to this, nothing but plain onriness and a dirty rat getting it in the neck where he had it coming to him, as you will see when I get the first part explained right.

Things first begun to go sour between Duke and Lura when they put the cats in. They didn't need no cats. They had a combination auto camp, filling station, and lunchroom out in the country a ways, and they got along all right. Duke run the filling station, and got me in to help him, and Lura took care of the lunchroom and shacks. But Duke wasn't satisfied. Before he got this place he had raised rabbits, and one time he had bees, and another time canary birds, and nothing would suit him now but to put in some cats to draw trade. Maybe you think that's funny, but out here in California they got every kind of a farm there is, from kangaroos to alligators, and it was just about the idea that a guy like Duke would think up. So he begun building a cage, and one day he showed up with a truckload of wildcats.

I wasn't there when they unloaded them. It was two or three cars waiting and I had to gas them up. But soon as I got a chance I went back there to look things over. And believe me, they wasn't pretty. The guy that sold Duke the cats had went away about five minutes before, and Duke was standing outside the cage and he had a stick of wood in his hand with blood on it. Inside was a dead cat. The rest of them was on a shelf, that had been built for them to jump on, and every one of them was snarling at Duke.

I don't know if you ever saw a wildcat, but they are

about twice as big as a house cat, brindle gray, with tufted ears and a bobbed tail. When they set and look at you they look like a owl, but they wasn't setting and looking now. They was marching around, coughing and spitting, their eyes shooting red and green fire, and it was a ugly sight, specially with that bloody dead one down on the ground. Duke was pale, and breath was whistling through his nose, and it didn't take no doctor to see he was scared to death.

"You better bury that cat," he says to me. "I'll take care of the cars."

I looked through the wire and he grabbed me. "Look out!" he says. "They'd kill you in a minute."

"In that case," I says, "how do I get the cat out?"

"You'll have to get a stick," he says, and shoves off.

I was pretty sore, but I begun looking around for a stick. I found one, but when I got back to the cage Lura was there. "How did that happen?" she says.

"I don't know," I says, "but I can tell you this much: if there's more of them to be buried around here, you can get somebody else to do it. My job is to fix flats, and I'm not going to be no cat undertaker."

She didn't have nothing to say to that. She just stood there while I was trying the stick, and I could hear her toe snapping up and down in the sand, and from that I knowed she was choking it back, what she really thought, and didn't think no more of this here cat idea than I did.

The stick was too short. "My," she says, pretty disagreeable, "that looks terrible. You can't bring people out here with a thing like that in there."

"All right," I snapped back. "Find me a stick."

She didn't make no move to find no stick. She put her hand on the gate. "Hold on," I says. "Them things are nothing to monkey with."

"Huh," she says. "All they look like to me is a bunch of cats."

There was a kennel back of the cage, with a drop door on it, where they was supposed to go at night. How you got them back there was bait them with food, but I didn't know that then. I yelled at them, to drive them back in there, but nothing happened. All they done was yell back. Lura listened to me awhile, and then she give a kind of gasp like she couldn't stand it no longer, opened the gate, and went in.

Now believe me, that next was a bad five minutes, because she wasn't hard to look at, and I hated to think of her getting mauled up by them babies. But a guy would of had to of been blind if it didn't show him that she had a way with cats. First thing she done, when she got in, she stood still, didn't make no sudden motions or nothing, and begun to talk to them. Not no special talk. Just "Pretty pussy, what's the matter, what they been doing to you?"—like that. Then she went over to them.

They slid off, on their bellies, to another part of the shelf. But she kept after them, and got her hand on one, and stroked him on the back. Then she got ahold of another one, and pretty soon she had give them all a pat. Then she turned around, picked up the dead cat by one leg, and come out with him. I put him on the wheelbarrow and buried him.

Now, why was it that Lura kept it from Duke how easy she had got the cat out and even about being in the cage at all? I think it was just because she didn't have the heart to show him up to hisself how silly he looked. Anyway, at supper that night, she never said a word. Duke, he was nervous and excited and told all about how the cats had jumped at him and how he had to bean one to save his life, and then he give a long spiel about cats and how fear is the only thing they understand, so you would of thought he was Martin Johnson just back from the jungle or something.

But it seemed to me the dishes was making quite a noise that night, clattering around on the table, and that was funny, because one thing you could say for Lura was: she was quiet and easy to be around. So when Duke, just like it was nothing at all, asks me by the way how did I get the cat out, I heared my mouth saying, "With a stick," and not nothing more. A little bird flies around and tells you, at a time like that. Lura let it pass. Never said a word. And if you ask me, Duke never did find out how easy she could handle the cats, and that ain't only guesswork, but on account of something that happened a little while afterward, when we got the mountain lion.

A mountain lion is a cougar, only out here they call them a mountain lion. Well, one afternoon about five o'clock this one of ours squat down on her hunkers and set up the worst squalling you ever listen to. She kept it up all night, so you wanted to go out and shoot her, and next morning at breakfast Duke come running in and says come on out and look what happened. So we went out there, and there in the cage with her was the prettiest he mountain lion you ever seen in your life. He was big, probably weighed a hundred and fifty pounds, and his coat was a pearl gray so glossy it looked like a pair of new gloves, and he had a spot of white on his throat. Sometimes they have white.

"He come down from the hills when he heard her call last night," says Duke, "and he got in there somehow. Ain't it funny? When they hear that note nothing can stop them."

"Yeah," I says. "It's love."

"That's it," says Duke. "Well, we'll be having some little ones soon. Cheaper'n buying them."

After he had went off to town to buy the stuff for the day, Lura sat down to the table with me. "Nice of you," I says, "to let Romeo in last night."

"Romeo?" she says.

"Yes, Romeo. That's going to be papa of twins soon, out in the lion cage."

"Oh," she says, "didn't he get in there himself?"

"He did not. If she couldn't get out, how could he get in?"

All she give me at that time was a dead pan. Didn't know nothing about it at all. Fact of the matter, she made me a little sore. But after she brung me my second cup of coffee she kind of smiled. "Well?" she says. "You wouldn't keep two loving hearts apart, would you?"

So things was, like you might say, a little gritty, but they got a whole lot worse when Duke come home with Rajah, the tiger. Because by that time he had told so many lies that he begun to believe them hisself, and put on all the airs of a big animal trainer. When people come out on Sundays, he would take a black snake whip and go in with the mountain lions and wildcats, and snap it at them, and they would snarl and yowl, and Duke acted like he was doing something. Before he went in, he would let the people see him strapping on a big six-shooter, and Lura got sorer by the week.

For one thing, he looked so silly. She couldn't see nothing to going in with the cats, and specially she couldn't see no sense in going in with a whip, a six-shooter, and a ten-gallon hat like them cow people wears. And for another thing, it was bad for business. In the beginning, when Lura would take the customers' kids out and make out the cat had their finger, they loved it, and they loved it still more when the little mountain lions come and they had spots and would push up their ears to be scratched. But when Duke started that stuff with the whip it scared them to death, and even the fathers and mothers was nervous, because there was the gun and they didn't know what would happen next. So business begun to fall off.

And then one afternoon he put down a couple of drinks and figured it was time for him to go in there with Rajah. Now it had took Lura one minute to tame Roger. She was in there sweeping out his cage one morning when Duke was away, and when he started sliding around on his belly he got a bucket of water in the face, and that was that. From then on he was her cat. But what happened when Duke tried to tame him was awful. The first I knew he was up to was when he made a speech to the people from the mountain-lion cage telling them not to go away yet, there was more to come. And when he come out he headed over to the tiger.

"What's the big idea?" I says. "What you up to now?"

"I'm going in with that tiger," he says. "It's got to be done, and I might as well do it now."

"Why has it got to be done?" I says.

He looked at me like as though he pitied me.

"I guess there's a few things about cats you don't know yet," he says. "You got a tiger on your hands, you got to let him know who's boss, that's all."

"Yeah?" I says. "And who *is* boss?"

"You see that?" he says, and cocks his finger at his face.

"See what?" I says.

"The human eye," he says. "The human eye, that's all. A cat's afraid of it. And if you know your business, you'll keep him afraid of it. That's all I'll use, the human eye. But of course, just for protection, I've got these too."

"Listen, sweetheart," I says to him. "If you give me a choice between the human eye and a Bengal tiger, which one I got the most fear of, you're going to see a guy getting a shiner ever time. If I was you, I'd lay off that cat."

He didn't say nothing: hitched up his holster, and went in. He didn't even get a chance to unlimber his whip. That tiger, soon as he saw him, begun to move around in a way that made your blood run cold. He didn't make for Duke first, you understand. He slid over, and in a second he was between Duke and the gate. That's one thing about a tiger you better not forget if you ever meet one. He can't work examples in arithmetic, but when it comes to the kind of brains that mean meat, he's the brightest boy in the class and then some. He's born knowing more about cutting off a retreat than you'll ever know, and his legs do it for him, just automatic, so his jaws will be free for the main business of the meeting.

Duke backed away, and his face was awful to see. He was straining every muscle to keep his mouth from sliding down in his collar. His left hand fingered the whip a little, and his right pawed around, like he had some idea of drawing the gun. But the tiger didn't give him time to make up his mind what his idea was, if any.

He would slide a few feet on his belly, then get up and trot a step or two, then slide on his belly again. He didn't make no noise, you understand. He wasn't telling Duke, "Please go away;" he meant to kill him, and a killer don't generally make no more fuss than he has to. So for a few seconds you could even hear Duke's feet sliding over the floor. But all of a sudden a kid begun to whimper, and I come to my senses. I run around to the back of the cage, because that was where the tiger was crowding him, and I yelled at him.

"Duke!" I says. "In his kennel! Quick!"

He didn't seem to hear me. He was still backing, and the tiger was still coming. A woman screamed. The tiger's head went down, he crouched on the ground, and tightened every muscle. I knew what that meant. Everybody knew what it meant, and specially Duke knew what it meant. He made a funny sound in his throat, turned, and ran.

That was when the tiger sprung. Duke had no idea where he was going, but when he turned he fell through the trap door and I snapped it down. The tiger hit it so hard I thought it would split. One of Duke's legs was out, and the tiger was on it in a flash, but all he got on the grab was the sole of Duke's shoe. Duke got his leg in somehow and I jammed the door down tight.

It was a sweet time at supper that night. Lura didn't see this here, because she was busy in the lunchroom when it happened, but them people had talked on their way out, and she knowed all about it. What she said was plenty. And Duke, what do you think he done? He passed it off like it wasn't nothing at all. "Just one of them things you got to expect," he says. And then he let on he knowed what he was doing all the time, and the only lucky part of it was that he didn't have to shoot a valuable animal like Rajah was. "Keep cool, that's the main thing," he says. "A thing like that can happen now and then, but never let a animal see you excited."

I heard him, and I couldn't believe my ears, but when I looked at Lura I jumped. I think I told you she wasn't hard to look at. She was a kind of medium size, with a shape that would make a guy leave his happy home, sunburned all over, and high cheekbones that give her eyes a funny slant. But her eyes was narrowed down to slits, looking at Duke, and they shot green where the light hit them, and it come over me all of a sudden that she looked so much like Rajah, when he was closing in on Duke in the afternoon, that she could of been his twin sister.

Next off, Duke got it in his head he was such a big cat man now that he had to go up in the hills and do some trapping. Bring in his own stuff, he called it.

I didn't pay much attention to it at the time. Of course, he never brought in no stuff, except a couple or raccoons that he probably bought down the road for two dollars, but Duke was the kind of a guy that every once in a while has to sit on a rock and fish, so when he loaded up the flivver and blew, it wasn't nothing you would get excited about. Maybe I didn't really care what he was up to, because it was pretty nice, running the place with Lura with him out of the way, and I didn't ask no questions. But it was more to it than cats or 'coons or fish, and Lura knowed it, even if I didn't.

Anyhow, it was while he was away on one of them trips of his that Wild Bill Smith, the Texas Tornado, showed up. Bill was a snake doctor. He had a truck, with his picture painted on it, and two or three boxes of old rattlesnakes with their teeth pulled out, and he sold snake oil that would cure what ailed you, and a Indian herb medicine that would do the same. He was a fake, but he was big and brown and had white teeth, and I guess he really wasn't no bad guy. The first I seen of him was when he drove up in his truck, and told me to gas him up and look at his tires. He had a bum differential that made a funny rattle, but he said never mind and went over to the lunchroom.

He was there a long time, and I thought I better let him know his car was ready. When I went over there, he was setting on a stool with a sheepish look on his face, rubbing his hand. He had a snake ring on one finger, with two red eyes, and on the back of his hand was red streaks. I knew what that meant. He had started something and Lura had fixed him. She had a pretty arm, but a grip like iron, that she said come from milking cows when she was a kid. What she done when a guy got fresh was take hold of his hand and squeeze it so the bones cracked, and he generally changed his mind.

She handed him his check without a word, and I told him what he owed on the car, and he paid up and left.

"So you settled his hash, hey?" I says to her.

"If there's one thing gets on my nerves," she says, "it's a man that starts something the minute he gets in the door."

"Why didn't you yell for me?"

"Oh, I didn't need no help."

But the next day he was back, and after I filled up

his car I went over to see how he was behaving. He was setting at one of the tables this time, and Lura was standing beside him. I saw her jerk her hand away quick, and he give me the bright grin a man has when he's got something he wants to cover up. He was all teeth. "Nice day," he says. "Great weather you have in this country."

"So I hear," I says. "Your car's ready."

"What I owe you?" he says.

"Dollar twenty."

He counted it out and left.

"Listen," says Lura, "we weren't doing anything when you come in. He was just reading my hand. He's a snake doctor, and knows about the zodiac."

"Oh, wasn't we?" I says. "Well, wasn't we nice!"

"What's it to you?" she says.

"Nothing," I snapped at her. I was pretty sore.

"He says I was born under the sign of Yin," she says. You would of thought it was a piece of news fit to put in the paper.

"And who is Yin?" I says.

"It's Chinese for tiger," she says.

"Then bite yourself off a piece of raw meat," I says, and slammed out of there. We didn't have no nice time running the joint *that* day.

Next morning he was back. I kept away from the lunchroom, but I took a stroll and seen them back there with the tiger. We had hauled a tree in there by that time, for Rajah to sharpen his claws on, and she was setting on that. The tiger had his head in her lap, and

Wild Bill was looking through the wire. He couldn't even draw his breath. I didn't go near enough to hear what they was saying. I went back to the car and begin blowing the horn.

He was back quite a few times after that, in between while Duke was away. Then one night I heard a truck drive up. I knowed that truck by its rattle. And it was daylight before I heard it go away.

Couple weeks after that Duke come running over to me at the filling station. "Shake hands with me," he says. "I'm going to be a father."

"Gee," I says. "That's great!"

But I took good care he wasn't around when I mentioned it to Lura.

"Congratulations," I says. "Letting Romeos into the place seems to be about the best thing you do."

"What do you mean?" she says.

"Nothing," I says. "Only I heard him drive up that night. Look like to me the moon was under the sign of Cupid. Well, it's nice if you can get away with it."

"Oh," she says.

"Yeah," I says. "A fine double cross you thought up. I didn't know they tried that any more."

She set and looked at me, and then her mouth begin to twitch and her eyes filled with tears. She tried to snuffle them up but it didn't work. "It's not any double cross," she says. "That night, I never went out there. And I never let anybody in. I was supposed to go away with him that night, but—"

She broke off and begin to cry. I took her in my

arms. "But then you found this out?" I says. "Is that it?" She nodded her head. It's awful to have a pretty woman in your arms that's crying over somebody else.

From then on, it was terrible. Lura would go along two or three days pretty nice, trying to like Duke again on account of the baby coming, but then would come a day when she looked like some kind of a hex, with her eyes all sunk in so you could hardly see them at all, and not a word out of her.

Them bad days, anyhow when Duke wasn't around, she would spend with the tiger. She would set and watch him sleep, or maybe play with him, and he seemed to like it as much as she did. He was young when we got him, and mangy and thin, so you could see his slats. But now he was about six years old, and had been fed good, so he had got his growth and his coat was nice, and I think he was the biggest tiger I ever seen. A tiger, when he is really big, is a lot bigger than a lion, and sometimes when Rajah would be rubbing around Lura, he looked more like a mule than a cat.

His shoulders come up above her waist, and his head was so big it would cover both her legs when he put it in her lap. When his tail would go sliding past her it looked like some kind of a constrictor snake. His teeth were something to make you lie awake nights. A tiger has the biggest teeth of any cat, and Rajah's must have been four inches long, curved like a cavalry sword, and ivory white. They were the most murderous-looking fangs I ever set eyes on.

When Lura went to the hospital it was a hurry call, and she didn't even have time to get her clothes together. Next day Duke had to pack her bag, and he was strutting around, because it was a boy, and Lura had named him Ron. But when he come out with the bag he didn't have much of a strut. "Look what I found," he says to me, and fishes something out of his pocket. It was the snake ring.

"Well?" I says. "They sell them in any ten-cent store."

"H'm," he says, and kind of weighed the ring in his hand. That afternoon, when he come back, he says: "Ten-cent store, hey? I took it to a jeweler today, and he offered me two hundred dollars for it."

"You ought to sold it," I says. "Maybe save you bad luck."

Duke went away again right after Lura come back, and for a little while things was all right. She was crazy about the little boy, and I thought he was pretty cute myself, and we got along fine. But then Duke come back and at lunch one day he made a crack about the ring. Lura didn't say nothing, but he kept at it, and pretty soon she wheeled on him.

"All right," she says. "There was another man around here, and I loved him. He give me that ring, and it meant that he and I belong to each other. But I didn't go with him, and you know why I didn't. For Ron's sake, I've tried to love you again, and maybe I can yet, God knows. A woman can do some funny things if she tries. But that's where we're at now. That's right where we're at. And if you don't like it, you better say what you're going to do."

"When was this?" says Duke.

"It was quite a while ago. I told you I give him up, and I give him up for keeps."

"It was just before you knowed about Ron, wasn't it?" he says.

"Hey," I cut in. "That's no way to talk."

"Just what I thought," he says, not paying no attention to me. "Ron. That's a funny name for a kid. I thought it was funny, right off when I heard it. Ron. Ron. That's a laugh, ain't it?"

"That's a lie," she says. "That's a lie, every bit of it. And it's not the only lie you've been getting away with around here. Or think you have. Trapping up in the hills, hey? And what do you trap?"

But she looked at me and choked it back. I begun to see that the cats wasn't the only things that had been gumming it up.

"All right," she wound up. "Say what you're going to. Go on. Say it!"

But he didn't.

"Ron," he cackles, "that's a hot one," and walks out.

Next day was Sunday, and he acted funny all day. He wouldn't speak to me or Lura, and once or twice I heard him mumbling to himself. Right after supper he says to me, "How are we on oil?"

"All right," I says. "The truck was around yesterday."

"You better drive in and get some," he says. "I don't think we got enough."

"Enough?" I says. "We got enough for two weeks."

"Tomorrow is Sunday," he says, "and there'll be a big call for it. Bring out a hundred gallon and tell them to put it on the account."

By that time I would give in to one of his nutty ideas rather than have an argument with him, and besides, I never tumbled that he was up to anything. So I wasn't there for what happened next, but I got it out of Lura later, so here is how it was:

Lura didn't pay much attention to the argument about the oil, but washed up the supper dishes, and then went in the bedroom to make sure everything was all right with the baby. When she come out she left the door open, so she could hear if he cried. The bedroom was off the sitting room, because these here California houses don't have but one floor, and all the rooms connect. Then she lit the fire, because it was cool, and sat there watching it burn. Duke come in, walked around, and then went out back. "Close the door," she says to him. "I'll be right back," he says.

So she sat looking at the fire, she didn't know how long, maybe five minutes, maybe ten minutes. But pretty soon she felt the house shake. She thought maybe it was a earthquake, and looked at the pictures, but they was all hanging straight. Then she felt the house shake again. She listened, but it wasn't no truck outside that would cause it, and it wouldn't be no state-road blasting or nothing like that at that time of night. Then she felt it shake again, and this time it shook in a regular movement, one, two, three, four, like that. And then all of a sudden she knew what it was, why Duke had acted so funny all day, why he had sent me off for the oil, why he had left the door open, and all the rest of it. There was five hundred pounds of cat walking through the house, and Duke had turned him loose to kill her.

She turned around, and Rajah was looking at her, not five foot away. She didn't do nothing for a minute, just set there thinking what a boob Duke was to figure on the tiger doing his dirty work for him, when all the time she could handle him easy as a kitten, only Duke didn't know it. Then she spoke. She expected Rajah to come and put his head in her lap, but he didn't. He stood there and growled, and his ears flattened back. That scared her, and she thought of the baby. I told you a tiger has that kind of brains. It no sooner went through her head about the baby than Rajah knowed she wanted to get to that door, and he was over there before she could get out of the chair.

He was snarling in a regular roar now, but he hadn't got a whiff of the baby yet, and he was still facing Lura. She could see he meant business. She reached in the fireplace, grabbed a stick that was burning bright, and walked him down with it. A tiger is afraid of fire, and she shoved it right in his eyes. He backed past the door, and she slid in the bedroom. But he was right after her, and she had to hold the stick at him with one hand and grab the baby with the other.

But she couldn't get out. He had her cornered, and he was kicking up such an awful fuss she knowed the stick wouldn't stop him for long. So she dropped it, grabbed up the baby's covers, and threw them at his head. They went wild, but they saved her just the same. A tiger, if you throw something at him with a human smell, will generally jump on it and bite at it before he does anything else, and that's what he done now. He jumped so hard the rug went out from under him, and while he was scrambling to his feet she shot past him with the baby and pulled the door shut after her.

She run in my room, got a blanket, wrapped the baby in it, and run out to the electric icebox. It was the only thing around the place that was steel. Soon as she opened the door she knowed why she couldn't do nothing with Rajah. His meat was in there; Duke hadn't fed him. She pulled the meat out, shoved the baby in, cut off the current, and closed the door. Then she picked up the meat and went around the outside of the house to the window of the bedroom. She could see Rajah in there, biting at the top of the door, where a crack of light showed through. He reached to the ceiling. She took a grip on the meat and drove at the screen with it. It give way, and the meat went through. He was on it before it hit the floor.

Next thing was to give him time to eat. She figured she could handle him once he got something in his belly. She went back to the sitting room. And in there, kind of peering around, was Duke. He had his gun strapped on, and one look at his face was all she needed to know she hadn't made no mistake about why the tiger was loose.

"Oh," he says, kind of foolish, and then walked back and closed the door. "I meant to come back sooner, but I couldn't help looking at the night. You got no idea how beautiful it is. Stars is bright as anything."

"Yeah," she says. "I noticed."

"Beautiful," he says. "Beautiful."

"Was you expecting burglars or something?" she says, looking at the gun.

"Oh, that," he says. "No. Cat's been kicking up a fuss, I put it on, case I have to go back there. Always like to have it handy."

"The tiger," she says. "I thought I heard him, myself."

"Loud," says Duke. "Awful loud."

He waited. She waited. She wasn't going to give him the satisfaction of opening up first. But just then there came a growl from the bedroom, and the sound of bones cracking. A tiger acts awful sore when he eats. "What's that?" says Duke.

"I wonder," says Lura. She was hell-bent on making him spill it first.

They both looked at each other, and then there was more growls, and more sound of cracking bones. "You better go in there," says Duke, soft and easy, with the sweat standing out on his forehead and his eyes shining bright as marbles. "Something might be happening to Ron."

"Do you know what I think it is?" says Lura.

"What's that?" says Duke. His breath was whistling through his nose like it always done when he got excited.

"I think it's that tiger you sent in here to kill me," says Lura. "So you could bring in that woman you been running around with for over a year. That redhead that raises Rabbit fryers on the Ventura road. That cat you been trapping!"

"And 'stead of getting you he got Ron," says Duke. "Little Ron! Oh my, ain't that tough? Go in there, why don't you? Ain't you got no mother love? Why don't you call up his pappy, get him in there? What's the matter? Is he afraid of a cat?"

Lura laughed at him. "All right," she says. "Now you go." With that she took hold of him. He tried to draw his gun, but she crumpled up his hand like a piece of wet paper and the gun fell on the floor. She bent him back on the table and beat his face in for him. Then she picked him up, dragged him to the front door, and threw him out. He run off a little ways. She come back and saw the gun. She picked it up, went to the door again, and threw it after him. "And take that peashooter with you," she says.

That was where she made her big mistake. When she turned to go back in the house he shot, and that was the last she knew for a while.

Now, for what happened next, it wasn't nobody there, only Duke and the tiger, but after them state cops got done fitting it all together, combing the ruins and all, it wasn't no trouble to tell how it was, anyway most of it, and here's how they figured it out:

Soon as Duke seen Lura fall, right there in front of the house, he knowed he was up against it. So the first thing he done was run to where she was and put the gun in her hand, to make it look like she had shot herself. That was where he made *his* big mistake, because if he had kept the gun he might of had a chance. Then he went inside to telephone, and what he said was, soon as he got hold of the state police: "For God's sake come out here quick. My wife has went crazy and throwed the baby to the tiger and shot herself and I'm all alone in the house with him and — *oh, my God, here he comes!*"

Now that last was something he didn't figure on saying. So far as he knowed, the tiger was in the room, having a nice meal off his son, so everything was hotsy-totsy. But what he didn't know was that that piece of burning firewood that Lura had dropped had set the room on fire and on account of that the tiger had got out. How did he get out? We never did quite figure that out. But this is how I figure it, and one man's guess is good as another's:

The fire started near the window, we knew that much. That was where Lura dropped the stick, right next to the cradle, and that was where a guy coming down the road in a car first seen the flames. And what I think is that soon as the tiger got his eye off the meat and seen the fire, he begun to scramble away from it, just wild. And when a wild tiger hits a beaver-board wall, he goes through, that's all. While Duke was telephoning, Rajah come through the wall like a clown through a hoop, and the first thing he seen was Duke, at the telephone, and Duke wasn't no friend, not to Rajah he wasn't.

Anyway, that's how things was when I got there with the oil. The state cops was a little ahead of me, and I met the ambulance with Lura in it, coming down the road seventy mile an hour, but just figured there had been a crash up the road, and didn't know nothing about it having Lura in it. And when I drove up there was plenty to look at all right. The house was in flames, and the police was trying to get in, but couldn't get nowheres near it on account of the heat, and about a hundred cars parked all around, with people looking, and a gasoline pumper cruising up and down the road, trying to find a water connection somewhere they could screw their hose to.

But inside the house was the terrible part. You could hear Duke screaming, and in between Duke was the tiger. And both of them was screams of fear, but I think the tiger was worse. It is a awful thing to hear a animal letting out a sound like that. It kept up about five minutes after I got there, and then all of a sudden you couldn't hear nothing but the tiger. And then in a minute that stopped.

There wasn't nothing to do about the fire. In a half hour the whole place was gone, and they was combing the ruins for Duke. Well, they found him. And in his head was four holes, two on each side, deep. We measured them fangs of the tiger. They just fit.

Soon as I could I run in to the hospital. They had got the bullet out by that time, and Lura was laying in bed all bandaged around the head, but there was a guard over her, on account of what Duke said over the telephone. He was a state cop. I sat down with him, and he didn't like it none. Neither did I. I knowed there was something funny about it, but what broke your heart was Lura, coming out of the ether. She would groan and mutter and try to say something so hard it would make your head ache. After a while I got up and went in the hall. But then I see the state cop shoot out of the room and line down the hall as fast as he could go. At last she had said it. The baby was in the electric icebox. They found him there, still asleep and just about ready for his milk. The fire had blacked up the outside, but inside it was as cool and nice as a new bathtub.

Well, that was about all. They cleared Lura, soon as she told her story, and the baby in the icebox proved it. Soon as she got out of the hospital she got a offer from the movies, but 'stead of taking it she come out to the place and her and I run it for awhile, anyway the filling-station end, sleeping in the shacks and getting along nice. But one night I heard a rattle from a bum differential, and I never even bothered to show up for breakfast the next morning.

I often wish I had. Maybe she left me a note.

EVELYN ARTHUR St. JOHN WAUGH
(1903-)

. . . is the son of a London publisher and brother of novelist Alec Waugh. He served as a war correspondent in Abyssinia, later joined the Royal Marines, and finally became a major of the English Commandos during World War II.

Waugh was only 33 when he won the Hawthornden Prize for his biography of Edmund Campion. As a novelist and biographer he has gained fame for his brilliant satire in such books as Officers and Gentlemen, Men At Arms, Decline and Fall, *and* The Loved One.

Film versions of his novels have brought him popularity and wealth.

THE MAN WHO LIKED DICKENS

in a South American jungle

ALTHOUGH MR. TODD had lived in Amazonas for nearly sixty years, no one except a few families of Pie-wie Indians was aware of his existence. His house stood in a small savannah, one of those little patches of sand and grass that crop up occasionally in that neighborhood, three miles or so across, bounded on all sides by forest.

The stream which watered it was not marked on any map; it ran through rapids, always dangerous and at most seasons of the year impassable, to join the upper waters of the river where Dr. Messinger had come to grief. None of the inhabitants of the district, except Mr. Todd, had ever heard of the governments of Brazil or Dutch Guiana, both of which, from time to time claimed its possession.

Mr. Todd's house was larger than those of his neighbors, but similar in character—a palm thatch roof, breast high walls of mud and wattle, and a mud floor. He owned the dozen or so head of puny cattle which grazed in the savannah, a plantation of cassava, some banana and mango trees, a dog and, unique in the neighborhood, a single-barrelled breech-loading shot gun. The few commodities which he employed from the outside world came to him through a long succession of traders, passed from hand to hand, bartered for in a dozen languages at the extreme end of one of the longest threads in the web of commerce that spreads from Manáos into the remote fastness of the forest.

One day while Mr. Todd was engaged in filling some cartridges, a Pie-wie came to him with the news that a white man was approaching through the forest, alone and very sick. He closed the cartridge and loaded his gun with it, put those that were finished into his pocket and set out in the direction indicated.

The man was already clear of the bush when Mr. Todd reached him, sitting on the ground, clearly in a very bad way. He was without hat or boots, and his clothes were so torn that it was only by the dampness of his body that they adhered to it; his feet were cut and grossly swollen; every exposed surface of skin was scarred by insect and bat bites; his eyes were wild with fever. He was talking to himself in delirium but stopped when Todd approached and addressed him in English.

"You're the first person who's spoken to me for days," said Tony. "The others won't stop. They keep bicycling by . . . I'm tired . . . Brenda was with me at first but she was frightened by a mechanical mouse, so she took the canoe and went off. She said she would come back that evening but she didn't. I expect she's staying with one of her new friends in Brazil . . . You haven't seen her have you?"

"You are the first stranger I have seen for a very long time."

"She was wearing a top hat when she left. You can't miss her." Then he began talking to someone at Mr. Todd's side, who was not there.

"Do you see that house over there? Do you think you can manage to walk to it? If not I can send some Indians to carry you."

Tony squinted across the savannah at Mr. Todd's hut.

"Architecture harmonizing with local character," he said, "indigenous material employed throughout. Don't let Mrs. Beaver see it or she will cover it with chromium plating."

"Try and walk." Mr. Todd hoisted Tony to his feet and supported him with a stout arm.

"I'll ride your bicycle. It *was* you I passed just now on a bicycle wasn't it? . . . except that your beard is a different color. His was green . . . green as mice."

Mr. Todd led Tony across the hummocks of grass towards the house.

"It is a very short way. When we get there I will

give you something to make you better."

"Very kind of you . . . rotten thing for a man to have his wife go away in a canoe. That was a long time ago. Nothing to eat since." Presently he said, "I say, you're English. I'm English too. My name is Last."

"Well, Mr. Last, you aren't to bother about anything more. You're ill and you've had a rough journey. I'll take care of you."

Tony looked round him. "Are you all English?"

"Yes, all of us."

"That dark girl married a Moor . . . It's very lucky I met you all. I suppose you're some kind of cycling club?"

"Yes."

"Well, I feel too tired for bicycling . . . never liked it much . . . you fellows ought to get motor bicycles you know, much faster and noisier . . . Let's stop here."

"No, you must come as far as the house. It's not very much further."

"All right . . . I suppose you would have some difficulty getting petrol here."

They went very slowly, but at length reached the house.

"Lie there in the hammock."

"That's what Messinger said. He's in love with John Beaver."

"I will get something for you."

"Very good of you. Just my usual morning tray—coffee, toast, fruit. And the morning papers. If her ladyship has been called I will have it with her . . ."

Mr. Todd went into the back room of the house and dragged a tin canister from under a heap of skins. It was full of a mixture of dried leaf and bark. He took a handful and went outside to the fire. When he returned his guest was bolt upright astride the hammock, talking angrily.

". . . You would hear better and it would be more polite if you stood still when I addressed you instead of walking round in a circle. It is for your own good that I am telling you . . . I know you are friends of my wife and that is why you will not listen to me. But be careful. She will say nothing cruel, she will not raise her voice, there will be no hard words. She hopes you will be great friends afterwards as before. But she will leave you. She will go away quietly during the night. She will take her hammock and her rations of farine . . . Listen to me. I know I am not clever but that is no reason why we should forget courtesy. Let us kill in the gentlest manner. I will tell you what I have learned in the forest, where time is different. There is no City. Mrs. Beaver has covered it with chromium plating and converted it into flats. Three guineas a week with a separate bathroom. Very suitable for base love. And Polly will be there. She and Mrs. Beaver under the fallen battlements . . ."

Mr. Todd put a hand behind Tony's head and held up the concoction of herbs in the calabash. Tony sipped and turned away his head.

"Nasty medicine," he said, and began to cry.

Mr. Todd stood by him holding the calabash. Presently Tony drank some more, screwing up his face and shuddering slightly at the bitterness. Mr. Todd stood beside him until the draught was finished; then he threw out the dregs on to the mud floor. Tony lay back in the hammock sobbing quietly. Soon he fell into a deep sleep.

Tony's recovery was slow. At first, days of lucidity alternated with delirium; then his temperature dropped and he was conscious even when most ill. The days of fever grew less frequent, finally occurring in the normal system of the tropics, between long periods of comparative health. Mr. Todd dosed him regularly with herbal remedies.

"It's very nasty," said Tony, "but it does do good."

"There is medicine for everything in the forest," said Mr. Todd; "to make you well and to make you ill. My mother was an Indian and she taught me many of them. I have learned others from time to time from my wives. There are plants to cure you and give you fever, to kill you and send you mad, to keep away snakes, to intoxicate fish so that you can pick them out of the water with your hands like fruit from a tree. There are medicines even I do not know. They say that it is possible to bring dead people to life after they have begun to stink, but I have not seen it done."

"But surely you are English?"

"My father was—at least a Barbadian. He came to Guiana as a missionary. He was married to a white woman but he left her in Guiana to look for gold. Then he took my mother. The Pie-wie women are ugly but

very devoted. I have had many. Most of the men and
women living in this savannah are my children. That
is why they obey—for that reason and because I have
the gun. My father lived to a great age. It is not twenty
years since he died. He was a man of education. Can
you read?"

"Yes, of course."

"It is not everyone who is so fortunate. I cannot."

Tony laughed apologetically. "But I suppose you
haven't much opportunity here."

"Oh yes, that is just it. I have a *great* many books. I
will show you when you are better. Until five years
ago there was an Englishman—at least a black man,
but he was well educated in Georgetown. He died. He
used to read to me every day until he died. You shall
read to me when you are better."

"I shall be delighted to."

"Yes, you shall read to me," Mr. Todd repeated,
nodding over the calabash.

During the early days of his convalescence Tony
had little conversation with his host; he lay in the hammock staring up at the thatched roof and thinking
about Brenda. The days, exactly twelve hours each,
passed without distinction. Mr. Todd retired to sleep
at sundown, leaving a little lamp burning—a hand-
woven wick drooping from a pot of beef fat—to keep
away vampire bats.

The first time that Tony left the house Mr. Todd
took him for a little stroll around the farm.

"I will show you the black man's grave," he said,

leading him to a mound between the mango trees. "He was very kind. Every afternoon until he died, for two hours, he used to read to me. I think I will put up a cross—to commemorate his death and your arrival—a pretty idea. Do you believe in God?"

"I suppose so. I've never really thought about it much."

"I have thought about it a *great* deal and I still do not know . . . Dickens did."

"I suppose so."

"Oh yes, it is apparent in all his books. You will see."

That afternoon Mr. Todd began the construction of a headpiece for the Negro's grave. He worked with a large spokeshave in a wood so hard that it grated and rang like metal.

At last when Tony had passed six or seven consecutive nights without fever, Mr. Todd said, "Now I think you are well enough to see the books."

At one end of the hut there was a kind of loft formed by a rough platform erected in the eaves of the roof. Mr. Todd propped a ladder against it and mounted. Tony followed, still unsteady after his illness. Mr. Todd sat on the platform and Tony stood at the top of the ladder looking over. There was a heap of small bundles there, tied up with rag, palm leaf and raw hide.

"It has been hard to keep out the worms and ants. Two are practically destroyed. But there is an oil the Indians make that is useful."

He unwrapped the nearest parcel and handed down

a calf bound book. It was an early American edition of *Bleak House.*

"It does not matter which we take first."

"You are fond of Dickens?"

"Why, yes, of course. More than fond, far more. You see, they are the only books I have ever heard. My father used to read them and then later the black man ... and now you. I have heard them all several times by now but I never get tired; there is always more to be learned and noticed, so many characters, so many changes of scene, so many words ... I have all Dickens books here except those that the ants devoured. It takes a long time to read them all—more than two years."

"Well," said Tony lightly, "they will well last out my visit."

"Oh, I hope not. It is delightful to start again. Each time I think I find more to enjoy and admire."

They took down the first volume of *Bleak House* and that afternoon Tony had his first reading.

He had always rather enjoyed reading aloud and in the first year of marriage had shared several books in this way with Brenda, until one day, in a moment of frankness, she remarked that it was torture to her. He had read to John Andrew, late in the afternoon, in winter, while the child sat before the nursery fender eating his supper. But Mr. Todd was a unique audience.

The old man sat astride his hammock opposite Tony, fixing him throughout with his eyes, and following

the words, soundlessly, with his lips. Often when a
new character was introduced he would say, "Repeat
the name, I have forgotten him," or "Yes, yes, I remember her well. She dies, poor woman." He would
frequently interrupt with questions; not as Tony would
have imagined about the circumstances of the story—
such things as the procedure of the Lord Chancellor's
Court or the social conventions of the time, though
they must have been unintelligible, did not concern
him—but always about the characters. "Now why does
she say that? Does she really mean it? Did she feel
faint because of the heat of the fire or of something in
that paper?" He laughed loudly at all the jokes and at
some passages which did not seem humorous to Tony,
asking him to repeat them two or three times; and
later at the description of the sufferings of the outcasts
in "Tom-all-alones" tears ran down his cheeks into his
beard. His comments on the story were usually simple.
"I think that Dedlock is a very proud man," or, "Mrs.
Jellyby does not take enough care of her children."

Tony enjoyed the readings almost as much as he
did.

At the end of the first day the old man said, "You
read beautifully, with a far better accent than the black
man. And you explain better. It is almost as though my
father were here again." And always at the end of a
session he thanked his guest courteously. "I enjoyed
that *very* much. It was an extremely distressing chapter. But, if I remember rightly, it will all turn out well."

By the time that they were in the second volume

however, the novelty of the old man's delight had begun to wane, and Tony was feeling strong enough to be restless. He touched more than once on the subject of his departure, asking about canoes and rains and the possibility of finding guides. But Mr. Todd seemed obtuse and paid no attention to these hints.

One day, running his thumb through the pages of *Bleak House* that remained to be read, Tony said, "We still have a lot to get through. I hope I shall be able to finish it before I go."

"Oh yes," said Mr. Todd. "Do not disturb yourself about that. You will have time to finish it, my friend."

For the first time Tony noticed something slightly menacing in his host's manner. That evening at supper, a brief meal of farine and dried beef, eaten just before sundown, Tony renewed the subject.

"You know, Mr. Todd, the time has come when I must be thinking about getting back to civilization. I have already imposed myself on your hospitality for too long."

Mr. Todd bent over the plate, crunching mouthfuls of farine, but made no reply.

"How soon do you think I shall be able to get a boat? . . . I said how soon do you think I shall be able to get a boat? I appreciate all your kindness to me more than I can say but . . ."

"My friend, any kindness I may have shown is amply repaid by your reading of Dickens. Do not let us mention the subject again."

"Well I'm very glad you have enjoyed it. I have, too.

But I really must be thinking of getting back ..."

"Yes," said Mr. Todd. "The black man was like that. He thought of it all the time. But he died here ..."

Twice during the next day Tony opened the subject but his host was evasive. Finally he said, "Forgive me, Mr. Todd, but I really must press the point. When can I get a boat?"

"There is no boat."

"Well, the Indians can build one."

"You must wait for the rains. There is not enough water in the river now."

"How long will that be?"

"A month ... two months ..."

They had finished *Bleak House* and were nearing the end of *Dombey and Son* when the rain came.

"Now it is time to make preparations to go."

"Oh, that is impossible. The Indians will not make a boat during the rainy season—it is one of their superstitions."

"You might have told me."

"Did I not mention it? I forgot."

Next morning Tony went out alone while his host was busy, and, looking as aimless as he could, strolled across the savannah to the group of Indian houses. There were four or five Pie-wies sitting in one of the doorways. They did not look up as he approached them. He addressed them in the few words of Macushi he had acquired during the journey but they made no sign whether they understood him or not. Then he drew a sketch of a canoe in the sand, he went through some vague motions of carpentry, pointed from them to him, then made motions of giving something to them and scratched out the outlines of a gun and a hat and a few other recognizable articles of trade. One of the women giggled but no one gave any sign of comprehension, and he went away unsatisfied.

At their midday meal Mr. Todd said, "Mr. Last, the Indians tell me that you have been trying to speak with them. It is easier that you say anything you wish through me. You realize, do you not, that they would do nothing without my authority. They regard themselves, quite rightly in many cases, as my children."

"Well, as a matter of fact, I was asking them about a canoe."

"So they gave me to understand . . . and now if you have finished your meal perhaps we might have another chapter. I am quite absorbed in the book."

They finished *Dombey and Son;* nearly a year had passed since Tony had left England, and his gloomy foreboding of permanent exile became suddenly acute when, between the pages of *Martin Chuzzlewit,* he found a document written in pencil in irregular characters.

Year 1919.

I James Todd of Brazil do swear to Barnabas Washington of Georgetown that if he finish this book in fact Martin Chuzzlewit I will let him go away back as soon as finished.

There followed a heavy pencil X and after it: *Mr. Todd made this mark signed Barnabas Washington.*

"Mr. Todd," said Tony, "I must speak frankly. You saved my life, and when I get back to civilization I will reward you to the best of my ability. I will give you anything within reason. But at present you are keeping me here against my will. I demand to be released."

"But, my friend, what is keeping you? You are under no restraint. Go when you like."

"You know very well that I can't get away without your help."

"In that case you must humor an old man. Read me another chapter."

"Mr. Todd, I swear by anything you like that when I get to Manáos I will find someone to take my place. I will pay a man to read to you all day."

"But I have no need of another man. You read so well."

"I have read for the last time."

"I hope not," said Mr. Todd politely.

That evening at supper only one plate of dried meat and farine was brought in and Mr. Todd ate alone. Tony lay without speaking, staring at the thatch.

Next day at noon a single plate was put before Mr. Todd but with it lay his gun, cocked, on his knee, as he ate. Tony resumed the reading of *Martin Chuzzlewit* where it had been interrupted.

Weeks passed hopelessly. They read *Nicholas Nickleby* and *Little Dorrit* and *Oliver Twist*. Then a stranger arrived in the savannah, a half-caste prospector, one of that lonely order of men who wander for a life-

time through the forests, tracing the little streams, sift-
ing the gravel and, ounce by ounce, filling the little
leather sack of gold dust, more often than not dying of
exposure and starvation with five hundred dollars'
worth of gold hung around their necks. Mr. Todd was
vexed at his arrival, gave him farine and *tasso* and sent
him on his journey within an hour of his arrival, but
in that hour Tony had time to scribble his name on a
slip of paper and put it into the man's hand.

From now on there was hope. The days followed
their unvarying routine; coffee at sunrise, a morning
of inaction while Mr. Todd pottered about on the business of the farm, farine and *tasso* at noon, Dickens in
the afternoon, farine and *tasso* and sometimes some
fruit for supper, silence from sunset to dawn with the
small wick glowing in the beef fat and the palm thatch
overhead dimly discernible; but Tony lived in quiet
confidence and expectation.

Sometime, this year or the next, the prospector
would arrive at a Brazilian village with news of his
discovery. The disasters of the Messinger expedition
would not have passed unnoticed. Tony could imagine
the headlines that must have appeared in the popular
press; even now probably they were search parties
working over the country he had crossed; any day English voices must sound over the savannah and a dozen
friendly adventurers come crashing through the bush.
Even as he was reading, while his lips mechanically
followed the printed pages, his mind wandered away
from his eager, crazy host opposite, and he began to

narrate to himself incidents of his homecoming—the gradual re-encounters with civilization (he shaved and bought new clothes at Manáos, telegraphed for money, received wires of congratulation; he enjoyed the leisurely river journey to Belem, the big liner to Europe; savored good claret and fresh meat and spring vegetables; he was shy at meeting Brenda and uncertain how to address her... *"Darling,* you've been much longer than you said. I quite thought you were lost...")

And then Mr. Todd interrupted. "May I trouble you to read that passage again? It is one I particularly enjoy."

The weeks passed; there was no sign of rescue but Tony endured the day for hope of what might happen on the morrow; he even felt a slight stirring of cordiality towards his jailer and was therefore quite willing to join him when, one evening after a long conference with an Indian neighbor, he proposed a celebration.

"It is one of the local feast days," he explained, "and they have been making *piwari.* You may not like it but you should try some. We will go across to this man's home tonight."

Accordingly after supper they joined a party of Indians that were assembled round the fire in one of the huts at the other side of the savannah. They were singing in an apathetic, monotonous manner and passing a large calabash of liquid from mouth to mouth. Separate bowls were brought for Tony and Mr. Todd, and they were given hammocks to sit in.

"You must drink it all without lowering the cup.

That is the etiquette."

Tony gulped the dark liquid, trying not to taste it. But it was not unpleasant, hard and muddy on the palate like most of the beverages he had been offered in Brazil, but with a flavor of honey and brown bread. He leant back in the hammock feeling unusually contented. Perhaps at that very moment the search party was in camp a few hours' journey from them. Meanwhile he was warm and drowsy. The cadence of song rose and fell interminably, liturgically. Another calabash of *piwari* was offered him and he handed it back empty. He lay full length watching the play of shadows on the thatch as the Pie-wies began to dance. Then he shut his eyes and thought of England and Hetton and fell asleep.

He awoke, still in the Indian hut, with the impression that he had outslept his usual hour. By the position of the sun he knew it was late afternoon. No one else was about. He looked for his watch and found to his surprise that it was not on his wrist. He had left it in the house, he supposed, before coming to the party.

"I must have been tight last night," he reflected. "Treacherous drink that." He had a headache and feared a recurrence of fever. He found when he set his feet to the ground that he stood with difficulty; his walk was unsteady and his mind confused as it had been during the first weeks of his convalescence. On the way across the savannah he was obliged to stop more than once, shutting his eyes and breathing deeply. When he reached the house he found Mr. Todd sitting there.

"Ah, my friend, you are late for the reading this afternoon. There is scarcely another half hour of light. How do you feel?"

"Rotten. That drink doesn't seem to agree with me."

"I will give you something to make you better. The forest has remedies for everything; to make you awake and to make you sleep."

"You haven't seen my watch anywhere?"

"You have missed it?"

"Yes. I thought I was wearing it. I say, I've never slept so long."

"Not since you were a baby. Do you know how long? Two days."

"Nonsense. I can't have."

"Yes, indeed. It is a long time. It is a pity because you missed our guests."

"Guests?"

"Why, yes. I have been quite gay while you were asleep. Three men from outside. Englishmen. It is a pity you missed them. A pity for them, too, as they particularly wished to see you. But what could I do? You were so sound asleep. They had come all the way to find you, so—I thought you would not mind—as you could not greet them yourself I gave them a little souvenir, your watch. They wanted something to take back to England where a reward is being offered for news of you. They were very pleased with it. And they took some photographs of the little cross I put up to commemorate your coming. They were pleased with that, too. They were very easily pleased. But I do not suppose they will visit us again, our life here is so retired . . . no pleasures except reading . . . I do not suppose we shall ever have visitors again . . . well, well, I will get you some medicine to make you feel better. Your head aches, does it not? . . . We will not have any Dickens today . . . but tomorrow, and the day after that, and the day after that. Let us read *Little Dorrit* again. There are passages in that book I can never hear without the temptation to weep."

ALLAN VAUGHAN ELSTON
(1887-   )

... was born in Missouri. He became a civil engineer. During World War I, he was a Captain in the U. S. Army; in World War II, he served as Lieutenant Colonel in the Tank Destroyers. Elston had a deep interest in American history and has always done his own on-the-spot research. He has coupled this inquisitiveness with his writing talent to create over 300 short stories and novelettes.

Most of Elston's books have appeared in serial form in the New York Daily News Syndicate. *He has also written for* Colliers, This Week, Adventure, *and* Argosy.

Film and television versions of his stories shown on "Alfred Hitchcock Presents," the "Robert Montgomery Show," and "Playhouse of the Air" have brought him nationwide fame.

It took a women's cool head

and clear thinking to thwart

BLACKMAIL

THE WOMAN WAS BLONDE and attractively thirtyish. Her suit, handbag, and hat matched, rather startlingly, in a pale shade of green. She appeared at midnight at the Fowler Street taxi stand.

"Where to, lady?" the cab dispatcher asked.

"4422 Heliotrope Drive."

The dispatcher scribbled on his call sheet: "4422 Heliotrope; 12:01 A.M." He said to the fare, "Sit down and wait, lady. Be a cab here in a minute."

Only a few cabs operated from the stand after midnight. Shortly one of them drew up. The dispatcher called, "Take the lady to 4422 Heliotrope, Ed."

The woman got in and was driven to the address. It was in a moderately fashionable district and the house, at this hour, was unlighted. The woman got out, paid and tipped the driver. "You needn't wait," she told him.

She took three steps up the lawn walk, then stopped to fumble in her bag, as though for a latchkey. This gave the cab time to drive away. When it was out of sight she turned and walked rapidly up the street, not stopping until she arrived at her own apartment, a mile away.

A night later, at the same hour, she again appeared at the Fowler Street taxi stand. Again she taxied to 4422 Heliotrope Drive. Again, once the cab was out of sight, she walked directly home.

She repeated the operation on thirteen successive nights.

But on the fourteenth night she arrived at the taxi stand five hours early. Twilight hadn't yet faded. Again she was driven to 4422 Heliotrope. This time, after getting out, she was awkward in passing the tip, and the coin dropped on the cab floor. Searching for it delayed the cabman's departure long enough for the woman to reach the house porch and ring the bell.

John Norman heard his front door chimes ring just as his living-room clock struck seven. He was alone in the house. His wife had been out of town for two weeks, but was due home tomorrow. They hadn't needed a servant since Judy, their teen-age daughter, had gone away to boarding school.

John went to the door, opened it, and confronted a woman he'd never seen before. She was slim and blonde and green-eyed.

"I'm afraid I'm lost." She spoke in a tone of embarrassed apology. "May I look up an address in your phone book? I'm late for a dinner party somewhere in this neighborhood. I thought it was in this block, but—"

"Help yourself," John Norman broke in heartily. "The same thing happened to me once." He stood aside to let her come in. "The telephone's right in the alcove."

"Thank you so much." She went to the alcove, picked up the phone book, and began thumbing through it.

When she emerged she smiled gratefully. "I got the address from the book. It's not far. Thank you."

Then John Norman became aware that she was staring ruefully at smudges on her finger tips. It looked like garden mud. A similar smudge was on her handbag.

"Now, where," she exclaimed in dismay, "did I get that?"

He presumed she'd dropped the bag in crossing the lawn. Stooping to pick it up, she could have soiled her fingers.

"Which means I have to go clear back home." Her lips drooped in chagrin. "And I'm late already." She took a step toward the door, then turned to him appealingly: "Unless you'd let me scrub it off right here! Would you? It wouldn't take but a minute."

"Sure," John agreed cordially. "The powder-room's

right there." He pointed to a door at the back of the hall.

"I'm sorry to be such a nuisance." She went back and disappeared into the powder-room.

John Norman heard the tap running and the faint sounds of scrubbing. In a few minutes she came out. "You've been awfully kind. Thanks again," she said.

She left the house. John Norman heard her heels click to the street walk. He dismissed her from his mind.

It was a busy mind. Currently the youngest and most energetic mayor in the history of this city, at the coming election John Norman was running for Congress. . . .

In the morning he drove to the airport to meet his wife.

Edith Norman uptilted her small dark face to be kissed. "I hope you've been lonesome every minute, darling," she said.

"Every minute," he assured her.

Edith had warm brown eyes and looked younger than most women of thirty-five. She was fiercely proud of her husband. A year from now they'd be living in Washington.

"I didn't forget to water the geraniums," John boasted. "And I sent Judy her allowance."

After taking Edith home he drove directly to his City Hall office. The day was filled with hearings, dictations, conferences, and the endless petitions likely to be born in a city of 200,000 people. Strings pulling first this way, then that. It was late afternoon before John found time for a huddle with Pete Delby, who was managing the congressional campaign. With Delby he formulated an answer to a charge made in J. Harrison Hardesty's opposition paper, the *Clarion*.

John was home by six, tired and hungry.

Edith met him at the door. "Why didn't you tell me you had a party while I was gone?" she chided him.

"I didn't."

"Then how did this"—Edith held up a solid gold compact with the initials "CG" on it—"get into the powder room?"

John hefted it curiously. "If gold's worth thirty-five an ounce, this must have set somebody back real dough. In the powder-room, you say?"

"It wasn't there," Edith said, "when I went away two weeks ago."

Then he remembered. "A woman," he explained, "came in to use the phone. She had mud on her fingers—"

"Begin at the beginning, please. What woman? She's a blonde. I can tell from the powder."

John gave every detail he could recall.

"Where," Edith questioned, "was the dinner party?"

"What dinner party?"

"The one she was on her way to when she got lost."

"How would *I* know?"

Edith looked thoughtful all through supper. Later she scanned the society page of the evening paper, line by line. "It doesn't mention any party last night in this neighborhood."

John settled back comfortably with his pipe. "So what. Lots of small, informal dinners don't get into the papers. The only funny thing is—why hasn't she come back for it? That gold compact."

"Maybe she has."

The constraint in Edith's voice made John look up. "You mean she did? Then why didn't you give it back to her?"

"I mean," Edith told him, "that twice today the telephone rang. I answered it each time. There was a pause. Followed by a faint feminine murmur: 'Sorry; wrong number.' Then a click as she hung up."

John shrugged. "People call wrong numbers all the time. Feel like taking in a show, Edie?"

She didn't.

It hardly began to strike John Norman as anything serious until he came home from the office an evening later. Edith didn't meet him at the door. He found her in the sun parlor looking very tense.

"CG called up again," she informed him.

"You mean Green-Eyes? What did she say?"

"When she heard *my* voice answer she purred, as usual, 'Sorry; wrong number.'"

John reddened. "See here, Edie. We've been married fifteen years. Don't you trust me? You think Green-Eyes is waiting to hear *my* voice answer the phone and then say, 'Hide that compact before your wife finds it'?"

Tears welled in Edith's eyes. She turned impulsively to John and put her arms around him. "She *wants* me

to think that. Don't you see? If she were really trying
to get in touch with you she'd call you at your office.
Not at home in the daytime, where you wife's almost
sure to answer. Then, by stealthily hanging up, she
makes herself sound guilty and mysterious."

It was a sobering thought. "It could be a smear
trick," John said.

"Of course it could. You're running for Congress.
She'd know from the society pages just when I left
town, and for how long. If she could make me accuse
you of having an affair while I was away, and it got
into the papers—"

"But you're *not* accusing me. And it won't get into
the papers. Anyway, the whole thing's fantastic. I
know my opponent, Lamson, wouldn't stand for a trick
like that. Neither would J. Harrison Hardesty, who's
backing him. Now, how about dinner, honey?"

At ten in the morning the secretary who screened
John Norman's appointments said, "A Miss Clara
Grant is on telephone number two, Mr. Norman. She
says it's personal."

The initials on the compact leaped into John's mind.
"I'll take it," he said tersely.

The voice on the phone spoke in the same tone of
embassassed apology he remembered: "I may have left
my compact at your house the other evening, Mr. Norman. Did you happen to find it?"

"I found a gold compact with 'CG' on it."

"Thank heaven!" she said. "I was afraid I'd left it in
a taxicab."

"Did you try to get me at my house?"

"Oh, no. It just this minute occurred to me I might have left it there."

"If you'll give me your address, Miss Grant, I'll see that you get it."

"Thank you so much. It's Apartment 1, 3306 Fowler."

She hung up, and John chuckled. So much for Edie's witchhunt suspicions! Trying to make something out of nothing. Clearly, Clara Grant was quite on the level.

But when he rang his wife to assure her of it, Edith was still doubtful: "Promise me you'll have someone check on her, John."

To please her, John promised. He sent for Dave Marcum, one of the abler plainclothes men on the city force.

Dave came in quietly and sat down. John gave him the known facts. "Now look, Dave. My wife suspects the compact was planted to smear me. I don't think so, but let's play it safe. I want you to go to 3306 Fowler, and find some excuse to talk to Miss Grant in Apartment 1. Size her up. Inquire around the neighborhood and make sure she's on the up-and-up. Find out of she has any political connections."

Dave Marcum's report, six hours later, dispelled the last shadow of apprehension in John's mind:

"Don't give it another thought, Mr. Norman. She *owns* that apartment building. It's a six-unit walk-up. She occupies one unit and lives off the rent from the other five. Crooks hardly ever own real estate. It keeps them from fading when they have to. As for politics, nobody in politics ever heard of this dame."

John hurried home to reassure Edith.

He didn't quite succeed. "I've still got my fingers crossed," she said stubbornly.

He took her in his arms. "But why?"

"Because I don't trust green-eyed blondes who borrow a married man's bathroom and then make pussyfooting calls to his wife."

John laughed. He pinched Edie's cheek and went to his den to work on the campaign speech he was to give the following night at Arlington.

Arlington was in a far corner of the congressional district. John caught a late afternoon train and went back to the parlor car. After making himself comfortable he closed his eyes and began mentally rehearsing his speech.

A voice startled him: "We can talk quietly here, Mr. Norman."

The blonde with the green eyes! Clara Grant. She had come into the car and taken the next chair.

"Well, Miss Grant," John said, "this is a surprise. I'm sorry I've not had a chance to return your compact. I planned—"

"That's not what I want at the moment," Clara Grant interrupted. Gone from her voice was the tone of apology. The green eyes had a predatory gleam.

"What *do* you want?" John asked cautiously.

"Twenty thousand dollars," she said.

John smiled grimly. "I suppose you also demand

that I withdraw from the congressional race?"

"You're quite wrong, Mr. Norman." The rumbling of wheels covered her voice. "I don't care who wins the election. All I want is twenty grand."

"A straight person-to-person shake-down. The answer is no. You've nothing on me. Even if you did have, I wouldn't pay you a dime."

"When you find out everything," she warned, "you may change your mind. If you don't, it'll be quite a shock to your wife."

John flushed. "Who put you up to this?"

"No one. I thought it out all by myself."

The train stopped at a station. In the comparative quiet Clara Grant lighted a cigarette and waited. When wheels began turning again she said, "I went to your house every night your wife was away. Always after midnight, except the last time. Those are the facts, and witnesses can prove them."

"Witnesses?" he asked.

"The witnesses," she asserted, "are all innocent, disinterested, and sincere. Now, about the pay-off, Mr. Norman. I'd rather not accept currency. You might try to trap me with marked bills."

"How else," John probed, "could I pay you twenty thousand?"

"I own the apartment house where I live. It's old and in need of repair, and on the present market won't bring more than fifty thousand. It's mortgaged for exactly that sum. I'm advertising it in the papers for seventy. You buy it for seventy. Which means you simply give me your check for twenty thousand and take title to the encumbered property. All done in the open, Mr. Norman, through any realtor you select."

That way, he saw, she'd be perfectly safe. Nothing to prove this conversation. If he accused her, it would be merely his word against hers.

"The deadline," she said coolly, "will be six P.M. of the Friday before election."

"I thought you said the election has nothing to do with it."

"The outcome hasn't. But the fact that you're running happens to make you a little more vulnerable.

John seethed. But surely it was just a bluff. How could she prove a series of midnight visits?

"Just what is your threat? If I don't pay before the election, what do you propose to do?"

"The opposition paper, Mr. Harrison Hardesty's *Clarion*," she said, "will receive an anonymous typed note. Apparently, it will come from a disgruntled taxi driver you had a row with one time. Actually, it will come from me. It will suggest that the *Clarion* take a look at the call sheets of the Fowler Street cabstand, with particular attention to a certain consistent midnight customer. The *Clarion* people want to defeat you, Mr. Norman. They'll start digging."

That evening at Arlington, John stumbled through his speech. It was the poorest effort of his career. When it was over he hurried to the station and caught a train back to his home city.

He arrived at midnight and got into a taxi. "Take

me," he directed grimly, "to the Fowler Street cab-stand."

A sleepy dispatcher was on duty there. He recognized John from campaign pictures in the papers and on billboards.

"I'm trying to check on one of your recent customers," John said. "Mind if I look at your call sheets for the last several weeks?"

"We don't keep a record of names, sir."

"I know. Let me see them, anyway."

The dispatcher pushed a dog-eared book toward John. The entries were in pencil. Each line had a destination and a time of departure. Nothing else.

John thumbed to the first date of Edith's absence from home. An entry said: "4422 Heliotrope; 12:01 A.M." On each of the next twelve nights he found a similar entry. A day later the record said: "4422 Heliotrope; 6:44 P.M.

That was all. He could see that the dispatcher was neither curious nor suspicious. It would be the same with the cabdrivers. To them 4422 Heliotrope was just another house.

But it would be different with smart reporters from the *Clarion*. Tipped to this record, they'd quickly identify the address as John Norman's. They'd question the dispatcher and the cabbies. A consistently repeating fare like Clara Grant would be remembered. They didn't know her name, but the fact of a series of midnight visits by a blonde would be established.

It could be a field day for the opposition and a hard-hitting sheet like the *Clarion.* From the first it had waged a no-holds-barred campaign against John.

John tossed the book back to the dispatcher. The taxi which had brought him from the station was still waiting. It did not operate from this stand. John rode home in it.

At breakfast he told Edith everything.

"It's a shakedown, Edie. She wants twenty thousand dollars."

For a bad moment he wondered if she'd doubt him. He could hardly blame her if she did. He was too proud to say, "She didn't really come in at midnight; she came only to the front walk." If Edie trusted him she'd have to figure that out herself.

He knew it was all right when Edith exclaimed bitterly, "She's a devil, that woman! I knew it all the time. Oh, John, what can we do?"

"Let's see if she really *is* running that ad."

John searched through the classified columns of the *Evening Tribune,* while Edith looked in the *Morning Clarion.*

It wasn't in the *Tribune.*

"Here it is in the *Clarion,*" Edith announced dismally. She read aloud:

" 'Just $70,000 for this lovely apartment of six compact units. Has every modern convenience. Hardwood floors throughout. BUY IT. Call Garfield 6600.' "

John looked up Clara Grant's number in the phone book. It was Garfield 6600.

"But you said *twenty* thousand, John," Edith exclaimed in confusion. "And the ad says *seventy*."

"The place is mortgaged to its full value, fifty thousand," John explained. "So I'd only have to raise twenty."

He drove dispiritedly to his office and sent for Dave Marcum. After bringing Dave up to date he said, "My only chance is to get the goods on her before the deadline. Get busy, Dave. I can't believe it's the first time she ever blackmailed anybody. Go back over her life. Find out whom she plays with. I want a microscopic report on her, and fast."

"Here's an angle," Dave suggested. "Maybe she's afraid the *Clarion* won't print that taxicab evidence without some solid charge to tie it in with. Like a lawsuit, or a street fight, or something."

"What do you mean?"

"I mean, suppose some man's in this with her. She gets him to punch you in the nose on the City Hall steps, him giving the taxicab visits for a motive. Or maybe the boy-friend beats *her* up, or pretends to, for the same motive. Or say she has a husband in the background who sues for divorce, naming you."

John shook his head bitterly. "You don't know the *Clarion*. It wouldn't wait for an excuse like that to smear me with every dirty straw in the wind."

The deadline was three weeks away.

At the end of the first week Dave reported, "I guess I was wrong, Mr. Norman. She's in this on her own, and I'll bet my badge on it. If she had a husband or a boy-friend or a lawyer working with her, I'd have turned him up by now."

"Dig deeper," John said. "Go farther back."

Another week dragged by. Clara Grant's ad continued to run every morning in the *Clarion*.

Then Marcum reported again. He looked more baffled than ever. "I still can't tie anything on her, Mr. Norman. She's played the stock market a few times, and lost, but who hasn't? All five tenants at her apartment house think she's on the level."

"Keep digging," John said.

He went into the last week of his campaign with a hopeless feeling. What good would it do? Before polling day he'd be head over heels in scandal. The *Clarion* would pounce on it. Of that he was certain. The cab-stand data was documentary evidence, and they'd use it with or without a boost from any other source.

The day of the deadline came: Friday before election. At eleven in the morning Clara Grant telephoned. Her voice said ominously, "You have seven hours, Mr. Norman."

Six of those hours slipped by and John went drearily home. Edith put her arms around him. "You've nothing to be ashamed of, John," she said.

"Lots of people," he told her, "will think I have. They'll whisper like witches."

"Let them," she said, with a lightness she didn't feel. She broke away and crossed to the fireplace. She picked up the gold compact from the mantel. "I stopped in at Leighton's today, John."

"The jeweler? Was the compact bought there?"

"I don't know," Edith said. "I just figured that if it were bought in town it must come from Leighton's, it's such an expensive thing. I spoke to Mr. Craft, the man who sold us our silver. He said he thought the compact was specially made. He found a tiny registration number in the lid, and he said he would check through the files and call me. If we can find out who bought the compact, maybe—"

"How did you tell him you got hold of it?" John asked anxiously.

"I said I found it and wanted to return it to its owner."

"But he hasn't called you?"

"No." Edith's voice was dejected. "He hasn't called."

They were both watching the living-room clock when it struck six.

"The deadline," John said.

Exactly an hour later the door chimes sounded. John went to the door. The man he saw on the front porch was slight and gray. John didn't invite him in.

"What do you want, Crowder?" John demanded.

Joshua Crowder was no mere reporter for the *Clarion*. He was the managing editor himself. Just now he seemed mild and inoffensive. But John knew he was tricky and craftily ambitious. He'd go the limit in polishing an apple for his boss and owner, J. Harrison Hardesty.

The man produced a typed note. "It's a copy," he announced, "of one somebody dropped on the city desk at six o'clock. Any comment, Mr. Mayor?"

John read it. Its wording ruthlessly fulfilled Clara Grant's threat. Her name wasn't on it. It might have come from a taxi driver with a grudge.

Crowder was too smart a newspaperman not to have stopped by the cabstand on the way here. Beyond doubt he'd copied down the cab-book entries and interviewed the dispatcher and a few cabbies.

"They all describe the same woman," he said, with a studied innocence. "How do you explain it, Mr. Mayor?"

"How would *you* explain it?"

"Obviously," Crowder said with a disarming candor, "it's a crude attempt at blackmail."

"Obviously," John echoed, so harassed that he failed to see the trap.

"Ah!" Crowder exclaimed, his eyes lighting. "Blackmail!" He was thinking in headlines already. "Have you anything to add? We'll have to cover it, of course, in our Bulldog edition."

"That's all." John closed the door and turned to Edith.

Her face was distraught. "But you shouldn't have admitted it was blackmail, John."

"Why not? It's the truth."

"But don't you see? Now you've given him a clear track. He won't even have to bother about ethics."

John laughed scornfully. "He wouldn't let ethics stop him. Not Crowder. It's just the chance he's been waiting for to get in solid with Old Man Hardesty."

He went to the telephone and called Pete Delby. "We're on a spot, Pete. The *Clarion's* printing a smear story. It's a frame, but it's dynamite. Meet me at campaign headquarters, Pete, and we'll hold a wake over it. And maybe you'd better round up some of our friends from the *Tribune.*"

After he'd gone Edith Norman reviewed the situation in a mood of despair. In less than five hours that hideous story would be public gossip. It would wreck John's career.

Clara Grant! What did they know about the woman. What could they prove? Nothing, except that she owned an apartment house which she was advertising for $70,000. Every morning Edith had seen the ad in the *Clarion.* A brazen demand, and yet what a cunning cover-up! If John paid her price it would be no more incriminating than if he'd responded to any other ad in the column.

Desolate and restless, Edith picked up the last issue of the *Clarion* and was reading the ad again, when the phone rang.

"Mrs. Norman?" a cultured masculine voice inquired.

"Yes," Edith said.

"This is Mr. Craft, of Leighton's, Mrs. Norman. I must humbly apologize for not having called you sooner about the owner of the compact. It slipped my mind completely. It wasn't until I got home that I realized—"

"That's quite all right," Edith interrupted. "You are

very kind to take the trouble. Did you find—?"

"No trouble at all, I assure you, Mrs. Norman. Any time Leighton's can be of service to you or the Mayor we will be proud—"

"Thank you, Mr. Craft. Did you find the owner? Was it one of your compacts?"

"Oh, yes, indeed, it is one of ours. And a very beautiful piece of work, if I may say so. It was especially executed for Mr. Hardesty—J. Harrison Hardesty. Mrs. Hardesty will be most grateful that someone of your honesty—"

"But the initials—" Edith began. Then she paused, a chill running through her.

"I beg your pardon," Mr. Craft said.

"You have been more helpful than I can tell you, Mr. Craft. I am indebted to you."

Mr. Craft laughed with derision. "It is we who are indebted to you, Mrs. Norman. Any time Leighton's can—"

"Yes, thank you," Edith said. She hung up slowly. Her mind raced from one thought to another, incapable of grasping the real meaning of this unexpected revelation.

She stared, unseeing, at the ad; then her eyes focused:

"Just $70,000 for this lovely apartment of six compact units. Has every modern convenience. Hardwood floors throughout. BUY IT! Call Garfield 6600."

From the first she'd noted the word "compact," a subtly insidious reminder to her victim. But now, reading the ad again, Edith saw something else. Reading only the capitals, she saw that the ad said:

JHH BUY IT! CG.

JHH stood for J. Harrison Hardesty, owner of the *Clarion*.

Downtown at campaign headquarters, John Norman and his brain trust were sweating it out. Pete Delby was there, swathed in gloom, as was Sam Casey of the friendly *Tribune*.

"When it hits the street," Pete Delby mourned, "we're washed up."

Casey was grimly practical: "Your wife's right, John. You opened the door wide for him when you admitted it was blackmail. Beginning with that as a legitimate news sensation, he can drag in the whole mess. When dog bites mayor, it's news. And editorially he can even be adroit, if he wants to: "We hope our distinguished mayor will quickly clarify his allegation. In spite of the evidence, reproduced impartially on page one of this issue, it seems incredible that—' "

Ted Porter, a *Tribune* leg man, came in. They'd sent Porter on a scouting tour to the *Clarion*.

Porter stated, "I happened to owe Chet Wilson, their chief proofreader, a sawbuck. So I dropped in to pay him off just as he was reading proof for the Bulldog edition. He got rid of me before I could see anything but a headline: 'MAYOR ALLEGES BLACKMAIL.' It's a three-column spread, Sam."

Casey looked sourly at his watch. It was ten o'clock. "In just two hours, John, your name's mud."

In the drawing-room of one of the more pretentious homes in the city, J. Harrison Hardesty sat facing a determined woman.

"You contradict yourself, Mrs. Norman," he protested. "First you say she's trying to make your husband buy a property for twenty thousand more than it's worth. Then you say she's trying to make *me* buy it."

"On the surface," Edith agreed, "it doesn't seem to make sense. Still, 'JHH BUY IT CG' either means she has something on you, or else it's a coincidence. I don't believe in coincidences, Mr. Hardesty. I think she made the demand of you, before she ever thought of my husband, and you turned her down."

"Then why," Hardesty refuted, "didn't she shoot her bolt, if she had one?"

"That's the genius of it," Edith said. "The weakness of a blackmailer is that once he executes his threat he's disarmed. He can no longer hope to collect. That was Clara Grant's dilemma. How could she eat her cake and still have it? The answer was to shoot her bolt, not at you but at someone else. It would give you an object lesson. For a convenient alternate, she picked my husband. She framed him, and then made the same demand she'd already made of you. It doubled her motive, because he might even pay off. But her main target all the while has been yourself. Unlike my husband you're a deep reservoir of wealth which she hopes to dip into again and again."

Hardesty mopped his plump, damp face. "Is that all?"

"There's still the gold compact. It's too heavy and extravagantly expensive for a woman in moderate circumstances to buy for herself. So it was a gift from some man. What man? Yourself, of course. If it weren't, why would Clara so deliberately needle you with it in the ad, and emphasize the pattern by introducing it also into the parallel threat against my husband?"

"You're guessing," Hardesty said.

"No, I'm not, Mr. Hardesty," Edith said quietly. *"I know.* I know that you ordered the compact from Leighton's. It was made to a special design. And I can prove it. Clara can prove some things, too. She can tell tales to your wife—and prove them. In fact, that's the only real hold she has on you. Your fear of your wife's reaction."

Panic gripped him. He gave an uneasy glance upward, and Edith sensed that his wife was asleep upstairs.

"Isn't it a fact," she pursued, "that you married the Goddard fortune? And that your wife still controls the purse strings? She lets you write checks and give orders. But if she knew about Clara Grant she could put you out in the street."

"You mean," he gasped, "that you'll tell her?"

"It won't be necessary. I'll make a trade with you, Mr. Hardesty. You take the *Clarion* off my husband's neck and I'll take Clara off yours."

He stared hopefully. "But how?"

"I assumed Clara doesn't know your wife's voice.

And I'm sure she doesn't know mine."

When Edith explained her plan, Hardesty jumped at it eagerly. Coached by Edith, he called Clara Grant on the telephone. He said to her, "I've told my wife everything, Clara. She knows—but here she is. She'll tell you herself." He handed the phone to Edith.

Edith spoke severely into the mouthpiece: "This is Mrs. Harrison Hardesty. Harrison has made a clean breast of his indiscretions, Miss Grant, and I intend to ignore the matter. But if you annoy him again, I'll personally prosecute you for blackmail."

She hung up with an arrogant snap and passed the telephone to Hardesty. "Your turn now. Call the *Clarion.*"

"Read it and weep!" Pete Delby mourned as he downed his fifth whisky sour. It was midnight at campaign headquarters and a boy had just delivered them the *Clarion's* Bulldog edition.

John Norman snatched it and looked at page one. The others bunched closely, staring fearfully over his shoulder.

"What is this?" Casey exclaimed. "You been kidding us?"

John turned to page 2, then to page 3, and on through the edition. Bewilderment shocked him. Nowhere was there any mention of himself, nor of a woman who took midnight rides in a cab.

But there was mention of John Norman the following Wednesday, and of his election to Congress. John and Edith sat together in their living-room and read the *Clarion's* full coverage of the victory.

Edith was glowing. She turned to John. "I think," she said, "this would be a propitious moment for us to have a few words from our new congressman."

John's eyes were bright. "No man," he said, "can more truthfully say, 'I owe my victory to my wife.' To her abundance of love, her abundance of trust . . ."

"And," Edith interrupted, laughing, "to her normal allotment of feminine curiosity."